"It couldn't have b
Us breaking up."

Seconds ticked by before Cliff nodded. "We were too young and we were pulled in different directions. Nothing you wanted was here."

"Except you."

"I felt the same about you."

"I'm sorry I was so hard on you."

"You had to be," he said. "You had to set us both free."

He brushed her hair back. "But it was perfect. Perfection is a rare thing. You don't find it often, and it seldom lasts. We were blessed."

He caught her face between his hands and kissed her. The way he had when the flame between them seared them with passion. She wanted this kiss more than anything, even though this was dangerous and they were still headed down separate roads. If ever the universe had decreed that a relationship wasn't meant to be, this was it.

So why couldn't she resist him?

* * *

Conard County: The Next Generation!

Dear Reader,

We all had a first love. If we were lucky, it turned out
well, or remained a good memory for us. But the
rivers of time keep flowing, and often we move on,
taking only our memories with us.

But there was something special about the first
love. Perhaps because we were young and so
full of hope, perhaps because it was the very
first. Regardless, it becomes an experience out of
time, full of a magic we hope we might find again
someday. Magic is certainly easier to find when
we're younger, but that doesn't mean we can't still
find it.

Writing this book gave me a marvelous opportunity.
Not many of us get a chance to revisit our first love
and remake it as the people we have become. In
Reuniting with the Rancher, two people who have
never forgotten their summer romance meet again.
There are some bad memories between them, and
a lot of lost time, but they find the magic once again,
this time on a firmer footing.

They have grown up, and so has their love. Enjoy!

Rachel

Reuniting with the Rancher

—

Rachel Lee

HARLEQUIN® SPECIAL EDITION®

Recycling programs
for this product may
not exist in your area.

ISBN-13: 978-0-373-65796-4

REUNITING WITH THE RANCHER

Copyright © 2014 by Susan Civil Brown

Printed in U.S.A.

RACHEL LEE

was hooked on writing by the age of twelve and practiced her craft as she moved from place to place all over the United States. This *New York Times* bestselling author now resides in Florida and has the joy of writing full-time.

Chapter One

Holly Heflin walked into the lawyer's office in Conard City with more uncertainty than she had felt in a long time, and she was used to facing some pretty ugly situations. But this was different—the reading of her great-aunt's will. She was, as far as she knew, the only heir, so her concern didn't lie there.

But she had arrived in Denver after a red-eye flight, hopped into the cheapest rental car she could find and driven straight here to make this meeting. She felt tired, grungy and most of all overcome by memory. Facing this meeting seemed so *final*.

Returning to Conard County wasn't easy, but she had the fondest memories of visits to her aunt's from childhood and early adulthood. They had begun washing over her from the instant the surrounding country began to look familiar, and with them came the numbness she had been feeling since the news of Martha's death had begun to give way to a deep well of grief.

The last of her family had died with Martha, and a sense of her solitariness in the world had been striking her in an utterly new way.

But she shoved all that down as she spoke to Jackie, the young receptionist. *Get through this. Get to the funeral home to watch Martha's ashes placed in a mausoleum.* Martha had always used to say she wanted to sprinkle her ashes around the ranch, but apparently that wasn't allowed, because the attorney had been quite definite, and Martha had paid all the expenses in advance.

God, the ache was growing. The reality was beginning to settle in, tightening her chest.

The receptionist ushered her into a spacious but ancient-looking office. She supposed the balding man behind the desk was the attorney, but then she saw the cowboy in one of the chairs facing the desk.

Her heart immediately jammed into her throat. Cliff Martin? Here? Of all the people on earth she never wanted to see again, he topped the list. She'd been busily burying her memories of him for nearly a decade now, trying to forget, trying to forgive herself. Apparently she hadn't succeeded.

He had always been attractive, but at thirty-two, Cliff Martin had become attractive to the point of danger. Weather and those ten years had etched themselves a bit on his face. Age had taken away any softness and his face now looked hard and chiseled. Those eyes were the same, though, an incredible turquoise that would make him a standout anywhere.

An instant shaft of remembered passion pierced her numbness, arrowing straight to her core and causing her insides to clench. She'd never wanted to see this man again, but apparently her body had other ideas. She glanced quickly away.

Both men rose immediately at her entrance, a courtesy that seemed quaint after the life she had been living. She tried not to look at Cliff, but couldn't help noticing that he seemed taller. Was that possible, or had her memory shrunk him? Broad shoulders, narrow hips... *Stop,* she ordered herself. *Just stop it now.* She didn't need this.

She immediately shook the lawyer's hand as he introduced himself. "John Carstairs," he said. "Good to see you, Ms. Heflin. And you remember Cliff Martin."

She turned to Cliff, wishing he didn't look as if he had just stepped out of a movie poster or ad. Darn, his dark hair didn't even show a thread of gray, unlike hers.

Cliff Martin. The man who had been helping her aunt keep the place up the past few years. The man who leased most of her aunt's grazing land. The man she had ditched. Her hand trembled a bit as she offered it.

He spoke. "So you finally got back here."

It sounded so much like a criticism that she had to bite back an angry retort. All she could do was drop her hand, turn away and take the empty chair. Working on the streets with troubled kids had taught her to be wary of how she responded to people. Problems could start in a flash.

She managed to keep her voice even. "I've been back."

The men sat. She avoided looking at Cliff Martin and focused on John Carstairs. "I traveled all night," she said. "I may be a little slow this morning."

He at once reached for his desk phone and punched a button. "Jackie? Could you bring some coffee for Ms. Heflin?" He arched a brow at her.

"Black, please."

"Make it black. Thanks, Jackie."

He released the button and sat back. Waiting. There was a strong sense of waiting, which made her even edgier after her race to get here. Then he said, "I'm sorry we had to meet under these circumstances. Your aunt was a wonderful woman."

"Yes, she was," Holly said honestly. "I'm going to miss her."

"Really," drawled Cliff.

At that she turned to stare at him. "How would you know? You know nothing."

"You haven't been around much."

That wasn't true, but again she bit back her retort. This man had no need to know anything, and she wasn't going to dignify his criticisms with explanations he had no right to.

"Please," said the lawyer, "let's be pleasant, shall we?"

Holly was all for pleasant. She was too tired for the spat Cliff apparently wanted. Jackie entered, setting a cup and saucer on the edge of John's desk in front of Holly. "Thank you."

Jackie smiled, nodded and walked out, closing the door quietly behind her.

John leaned forward. "As I told you, Ms. Heflin, your great-aunt made all the arrangements. They'll be waiting for you at the funeral home after we're done here. But there are other things we need to discuss."

"Yes," she said. There was also one thing she knew for sure, that a visit with a lawyer was supposed to be private. "But what is Mr. Martin doing here? You said I was Martha's sole heir."

"He," said John, "is the executor."

Holly's mind whirled. Maybe it was fatigue. Maybe it was burgeoning grief. All she knew was that she felt as if she had been sideswiped by a Mack truck. "Why not you?" she asked quietly.

"Conflict of interest. And it was your aunt's decision."

"Of course." She was still trying to take this in. She was going to have to deal with a man who had every reason to believe she was hateful? Well, it wouldn't be the first time. Still. She reached for the coffee and took a few sips, hoping to assemble her brain into a more orderly pattern than it seemed to be following right now. She noted that her hand trembled, and she quickly put the coffee down.

Deal. The word wafted up. She always dealt. Whatever life threw her way, she was good at it. She'd deal with all of this somehow, from grief to that nasty cowboy.

"I'm going to give you a copy of your aunt's will to read at your leisure. In the meantime, I'll just go over the broad aspects here."

"That's fine." She certainly didn't feel up to dealing with anything detailed.

"You've inherited the ranch. It's free and clear except for the leases. As the law makes clear, those leases to Mr. Martin remain in place, and your aunt's will states that he is allowed to continue leasing the land at his discretion for the next ten years."

Holly felt her heart began to sink. That meant she would have to deal with this ghost from her past indefinitely.

"Your aunt was also a very careful woman, and left you a great deal of cash, a quite surprising amount, actually. Mr. Martin has the necessary papers giving him management of the estate, and he'll take you to the bank to transfer the accounts into your name."

Holly managed a jerky nod. Nothing seemed to be penetrating except that she was now locked into some kind of long-term relationship with a man she had been avoiding for a long time. A man she had never wanted to see again. Martha had known that. What had possessed her aunt?

"In addition, you're not allowed to sell the ranch for at least ten years. But your aunt added something to that."

Holly lifted her head. "Yes?"

"She said to find your dream. I'm not sure what she meant."

Holly's heart rose, just a bit. God bless Aunt Martha, even though she didn't know what her aunt meant. "I'm not sure, either."

Carstairs shrugged. "Well, that's what she said, and if it has anything to do with the ranch, she made sure it would be possible for you. So those are the essentials. The rest is mostly legal stuff that you can call me about if you have questions."

Sooner than she would have believed, she was out of the office and back on the street. Downtown Conard City hadn't changed in any way she could perceive. It seemed to be cast in amber, preserved and unchanging. It had always charmed her, coming as she did from larger towns and cities, and she paused for a moment to soak it all in. There was a peaceful air to this place that had never failed to draw her during her visits. But since Cliff, she had never wanted to make this her home.

That wasn't likely to change. She started to turn toward her rental when Cliff's voice yanked her up short. "The funeral home is the other way."

She turned. "I know. I'm driving." What did he care?
"It's not that far. I'll see you there then."

He was going to be there, too? Somehow she had
imagined herself quietly putting her aunt to rest. But of
course Martha must have had friends. She looked down
at herself, at her overworn black sweater and slacks, and
wished she had thought this through. Surely she could
have dressed better for this?

God, all that had been on her mind was getting out
here in time. To do her last act for her beloved great-
aunt. She'd raced to find a plane ticket, fought to reserve
a rental car that wouldn't completely impoverish her,
put on something black and fled her dingy apartment.

Now she felt as dingy as the streets she had left behind.

She climbed into her car, found a brush in her purse
and ran it swiftly through her wavy chestnut hair. A
glance in the rearview mirror told her that her makeup
was long gone, not that she cared. Instead of primping
any more, she headed for the funeral home.

Inside she found her fears confirmed. Some forty
or fifty people milled about the place, and while she
couldn't remember any of them, they all seemed to
know who she was. She was quickly swamped in con-
dolences and a sea of names. Some offered a memory
or two of her aunt.

And with each memory her throat grew tighter. Soon
she could feel the sting of withheld tears in her eyes,
and wished only that this would be over so she could
get out to the ranch and cry in private.

God, she hadn't even had time to get some flowers.

None too quickly, the funeral director announced it
was time. The crowd followed him at a somber pace as
he carried Martha's urn through a door, across a cov-

ered walkway to a large concrete mausoleum. There, one door to a niche stood open and waiting.

Holly swallowed hard. She swallowed even harder when a man stepped forward and said, "I was Martha's minister for many years. I know she refused a memorial service, saying she only hoped that she would be well remembered. We remember Martha well indeed. A generous woman, with a kind heart. We are grateful she passed swiftly and without warning, and know that she rests now in God's love."

Then he insisted on reciting the Twenty-third Psalm. Before it was done, the unbidden tears were rolling hotly down Holly's cheeks. When the funeral director slid the urn into its niche, she stepped forward and laid her hand on it, not wanting to see it disappear, hanging on for one last moment.

"I love you," she whispered. Then she stepped back and watched the director close and lock the door. A brass plate on the outside listed Martha's name, her dates of birth and death. Nothing else.

When she turned she found all those people looking at her as if they expected her to speak. A moment of panic fluttered through her, memories surged, and then she remembered something her aunt had once said to her.

"Aunt Martha told me that she wanted to leave a small footprint in this world. That she wanted to leave the land as it was meant to be, and nearly everything as she had found it. Except for one thing. She hoped that she would leave small footprints in the hearts of her friends, and that they would bring smiles. Thank you all."

Then she pivoted to stare at that closed vault. Great-Aunt Martha was gone. The times between her visits had been punctuated by weekly phone calls with her aunt. Now there would be no more calls and it hit her: there was a huge difference between being separated by miles and being separated by death.

A huge, aching chasm of a difference.

Cliff Martin watched Holly Heflin with dislike. She was still a pretty sprite, with wavy auburn hair and bright blue eyes. He felt that all too familiar surge of desire for her and had to battle down memories of how her gentle curves had felt in his arms. But too much lay between them for him to like her. While Martha had defended Holly more than once, he had the wounds to show for how she had treated him. A long-ago summer affair, brief, fleeting, had left him an angry man for a long time and convinced him that Holly was as self-centered as a woman could be. Martha's talk of her youth hadn't helped one whit.

Regardless, now he was tied to this woman by Martha, who for reasons he couldn't begin to understand had made him executor of her will. Not that there was a lot to carry out. And there was Holly, a woman even more beautiful than at twenty, now part of his life again whether he liked it or not. He didn't like it.

What had Martha been thinking? He was grateful to her for protecting his leases. It would have killed his ranching operation to give up all that land. But what was with the ten years? And the stuff about Holly following her dream?

Not that he cared about Holly's dreams. Holly's dreams had nearly killed him once. To his way of thinking, she wasn't trustworthy. Maybe Martha felt the same, and had put the leases in her will to ensure Holly didn't kick him off the land. But damn, this was going to be miserable. He needed that woman like he needed a hole in his head.

But for all he had wanted to think Holly was an uncaring witch, nothing could make him believe those tears weren't real.

He didn't get any of this, but he supposed it didn't matter. Martha had gone her own way, quirky and delightful and always surprising. Why should she end her life any differently?

He watched Holly decline to go to the church for a covered-dish supper. Martha had wanted no memorial, but others were going to give it to her anyway. How that would have made her laugh.

But her niece seemed determined to follow her aunt's wishes. He watched her walk to her car, a slender woman with beautiful auburn hair and blue eyes, and thought how utterly alone she looked. And how very sexy. Since those thoughts had gotten him in trouble once before, he clamped down on them hard, and wished them to hell.

No way was he going to fall for that blue-eyed seductress again.

With any luck, Holly Heflin would blow back out of town as fast as she had blown in, taking whatever funds Martha had left her and leaving the ranch to rot. She was a city girl, after all.

He wondered if she'd let the house and barn turn to dust. He certainly wasn't going to do all the maintenance for her as he had done for Martha. He didn't owe her that and she wouldn't even qualify as a neighbor.

Damn, he felt angry for no reason that he could figure out. He'd had a low opinion about Holly for years, so no shock there. Absolutely no reason to be angry all over again.

Cussing under his breath anyway, he skipped the potluck and headed home. He had a ranch to take care of and only one task remaining as far as Martha went: to take her niece to the bank and see that the accounts got turned over to her.

And, he supposed, to ensure she didn't try to sell the ranch. It didn't look as if she would care, so what the hell.

Trying to get himself into a better mood, he turned on some music on the radio, discovered a sad country song and turned it off again.

Damn, he thought. "Martha, why do I get the feeling you left me a mess and I don't even know how bad it is yet?"

Of course there was no answer.

Holly arrived at the ranch with sand in her eyes and lead in her heart. She climbed out of the car and looked around, memories whispering to her on the breeze. As a child she had absolutely loved coming out here. As a young woman, after Cliff, the charm had rested entirely with her aunt's company.

Turning, she surveyed the changes. Cliff must have rented damn near all the land, to judge by how close the fences were now. But he'd also kept the place up for Martha, and sooner or later she was going to have to thank him for that no matter how the words stuck in her craw.

Memories wafted over her. She'd spent some summers here as a small child, then when she'd grown up her visits had been shorter because she had a job, but still she had come, for Martha. With one exception, every memory was good. Time and frequent visits, at least, had mostly cleared Cliff from her memories of this place. It almost seemed that only Martha remained here.

Great-Aunt Martha had been the kind of woman that Holly hoped she'd grow up to be: tough, independent, doing things pretty much her own way, but kind and loving to the core.

She made herself brush away her reaction to Cliff and climbed the steps of the porch to the front door. Her key still worked and she stepped into the past, into familiar smells that carried her back over the years, into familiar sights, into a place that had always been her second home.

In that instant, knowing she would never see Martha again, she burst into the tears she'd been trying to hold back.

She'd always felt close to Martha, despite the miles that had separated them for so long, and it hurt to realize she could never again pick up the phone and hear her aunt's voice.

Never again.

Keeping busy seemed to be the only answer. Holly was used to being busy all the time, and sitting around her aunt's house weeping and doing nothing went against her grain. Martha, thank goodness, hadn't been sick. She had died suddenly and unexpectedly of a stroke, a merciful way to go, for which Holly was grateful. But it also meant the house was in pretty good shape inside as well as out. Not a whole lot of housework to occupy her, other than putting away the groceries she had bought and changing bed linens.

That left going through things. Martha had been a minimalist most of her life, buying very little, keeping very little that she didn't use. But in going through drawers and looking at photos, Holly found plenty to carry her into memory. Pictures of her visits here, pictures of her parents, photos of Martha's own parents and grandparents. She wasn't awash in photos, as Martha hadn't been one for taking very many, but there were enough to be cherished.

The furnishings showed their age and use but were still serviceable. The house seemed to be ready for her, and she wondered if Martha had intended that. Maybe.

She certainly hadn't left any unfinished chores behind her.

Finally, unable to bear any more, she headed for the bedroom she had used during her visits. The big stuffed teddy bear Martha had given her as a child still occupied the rocker in the corner. Holly fell asleep hugging it and thinking of her aunt, the last of her family.

Morning brought no relief. Sleep had been disturbed, and she hardly felt any more rested than yesterday.

Then she remembered something Martha had been definite about. "You want to do something for me? Plant a tree."

So she decided, after choking down her breakfast, that today she would go find a tree to plant just for Martha. Its importance grew in her mind as she thought about it. Martha had wanted it, and Martha would get it.

After she finished washing her dishes, Holly gripped the edge of the counter, closed her eyes, and tried not to hear the empty silence of the house around her. She couldn't believe she wouldn't hear Martha's voice at any moment. Couldn't believe that Martha was really gone.

God, it was beginning to hit. Numbness had begun wearing off yesterday, but now it seemed to be deserting her completely.

Hot tears rolled down her cheeks, and her heart ached as if a vise gripped it. She had known it would hurt to lose her aunt, but she hadn't imagined this. It was every bit as bad as when her parents died in the car crash. Every bit, and that grief still haunted her.

Martha had been her anchor ever since, her family, the person who kept her from feeling like an orphan, and now Martha was gone.

Never had Holly felt so utterly alone.

She wept until she could weep no more, until fatigue weighed her down and her sides hurt from sobbing. But at last quiet returned to her mind and heart. Temporarily, anyway. She fixated on getting that tree, the one wish of her aunt's that she could still carry out.

She washed up, dressed in jeans and a hoodie, the clothes she wore when she was working with the children, and stared almost blindly at her reflection in the mirror.

Who was she? It almost seemed as if she had become a stranger to herself, as if grief were sweeping huge parts of her aside. Closing her eyes, she thought of the kids she worked with back home in Chicago, kids who were always hungry, often cold, flotsam in a sea beyond their control.

Thinking of them grounded her again, reminding her she had a purpose, and purpose was the most important thing of all.

When she finally stepped outside to face the day's duties, she paused in the drive, feeling the spring breeze of Conard County, Wyoming, whisper all around her. Here the air was almost never still, and it seemed to carry barely heard words on it, as if it were alive.

She opened herself to it, letting it wash over her like

a tender touch, the kind of tenderness she wouldn't feel again, the tenderness of mother, father, aunt.

She took time to walk around the house taking in the small changes, having random thoughts about what she could do with this place. Her job as a social worker lay back in Chicago, but as she strolled around she realized that an ever-present tension had begun to evaporate. Today she didn't have to walk on those streets; she didn't have to visit tiny apartments in public housing where despair seemed to paint the walls. She didn't have to deal with the problems of too-skinny children who were having trouble in school or at home. She didn't have to wage a battle against desperation and hopelessness. Not today.

Then, squaring her shoulders, she strode to the car. A tree. She needed to get a tree.

She saw a vehicle coming up her driveway. A dusty but relatively recent pickup of some kind. Who could possibly be coming out here?

She didn't have to wait long for her answer. She quickly recognized Cliff's silhouette behind the wheel. A few seconds later he pulled up beside her.

"Going somewhere?" he asked.

She resisted the urge to tell him it was none of his business, because she might have to deal with him for a long time to come. "My aunt wanted me to plant a tree in her memory. I was about to go look for one."

He glanced at her rental. "Hard to carry in that. I was coming if to see if you wanted to take care of the bank account transfer. The sooner we clear the decks, the happier we'll both be."

Her teeth tightened. He *really* wasn't going to let her forget. "Fine," she said shortly.

He looked at her car again. "You planning to stay long?"

"I have a couple of weeks before I have to get back. If that's long, then yes."

"One rain and that car won't get anywhere. You'll bog down."

"It's a rental," she said defensively, feeling as if he was criticizing her somehow. "Do you *ever* say anything that's not critical?"

He paused. "I call things as I see them. So did your aunt. How about you?"

"What I see is a man I intended to thank for helping Aunt Martha, but right now I couldn't choke the words out to save my life. You're rude."

His lips tightened, but his response was mild. "I see a little of your aunt in you."

She didn't respond. Ordinarily she would have taken that as a compliment, but right now she wasn't in the mood. Besides, with this man, it must have been a sideways condemnation of some kind. He had plenty of reason to hate her, she knew, but after ten years, shouldn't he be over it? Stupid question, she thought immediately. Her own behavior still troubled her after all these years.

"Well, climb in my cab. I can carry a tree in my bed better than you can in that car, and we can take care of the bank."

She wanted to refuse. Oh, man, did she want to tell him to take a hike, and even more so because of the antipathy that radiated from him. She was starting to feel a whole lot of dislike for him, too. Before, she'd never disliked him, but now she wondered if she had been more wise than foolish all those years ago.

Damn this unwanted sexual attraction. Any woman

would feel it, she assured herself. It was just normal. He was that kind of guy, a real-life hunk.

She didn't want it, though. Not one little bit. She'd tasted that apple a long time ago, and it hadn't been enough to keep her here. She'd grown up, but she was beginning to wonder if he had.

She had to give in to reality. He was right—carrying a tree would be easier in his truck.

Setting her chin, she marched around and climbed in the cab, prepared for a couple of unpleasant hours, not the least of which would be the way her body kept wanting to betray her mind and heart.

Chapter Two

As unneighborly as it felt, Cliff didn't say a word on the way to town. What were they going to talk about anyway? Discussing Martha didn't seem exactly safe right now, although maybe he was wrong.

On the other hand, he didn't want to renew his relationship with Holly. Not in the least. A summer-long torrid affair a decade ago had left him scarred and her... What had it done to her? She'd turned her back on him readily enough, giving him all the reasons why she couldn't stay in this county. She'd suffocate, she'd said. She had important things to do, she'd said. She was going to be a social worker and save the world, or at least part of the world.

He glanced at her from the corner of his eye and thought that social work didn't seem to be agreeing with her. She looked entirely too thin, for one thing. He couldn't judge anything else because she was griev-

ing for her aunt, after all, but if he'd been looking at
a horse showing those signs, he'd have been thinking
"worn to the bone."

Fatigue seemed to wrap around her. She didn't really have the spark he remembered. Much as he didn't
want to, he wondered if social work had gutted her in
some way.

But damned if he'd ask. She'd be leaving here in two
weeks. By the grace of heaven, he hoped that wouldn't
be long enough to open scars or get him all tangled up
in her barbed wire again.

Because that was how he thought of it: barbed wire.
Her departure had scored him deep, like a million sharp
knives. No freaking way was he going through that
again.

Of course, he thought, she might not be the same
person any longer. He might not even really be drawn
to the woman she had become. So far he hadn't seen
much to like. It was almost as if he were the enemy, not
the other way around.

Which got him to wondering how she had justified
her cruelty. Ah, hell, leave that can of worms alone.
Take her to the bank, help her buy and plant the damned
tree, and then forget she was on the same part of the
planet with him.

Listening to his own thoughts, however, yanked him
up short. He was thinking like a kid again. She was
causing him to revert. Well, to hell with that.

He was relieved the bank took only a few minutes.
He showed the paper the lawyer had given him, Martha's account was moved into a new one in Holly's name
and it was done.

Mercifully soon, they were climbing into his truck

again. Holly, however, seemed to sag. Finally he couldn't keep quiet any longer.

"What's wrong?"

"Did you see how much money she left me? Cliff… I'm stunned."

"Well, you could take a decent vacation. Looks like you need one."

She bridled, but only a bit, not as she once had. What the hell had quenched her fire? "That's more than a vacation or even ten. And what do you mean I look like I need one?"

"You look too thin and exhausted," he said bluntly. "Whatever kind of work you're doing, it's not good for your health."

"You don't know what you're talking about."

"I never did." He waited for an explosion that didn't come. Oh, this was bad. This wasn't the Holly he remembered at all. Now, right alongside his annoyance at having her around for a while, he felt the first tendrils of worry. Was she sick?

None of his business anymore, he reminded himself. She'd made sure of that.

The town didn't have anything like a big nursery. Around here, most planting was reserved for hay, alfalfa and vegetable gardens. But there was a corner at the feed store where it was possible to buy houseplants and some ornamental trees. Not a huge selection, but no huge demand, either. They *would* order stuff in, though, if, say, someone wanted to plant a windbreak or something bigger.

"What were you thinking of planting for her?" he asked as they stood looking at the tiny selection.

"Well, she always said she wanted to leave a small footprint in the world, so it should be something native."

He hesitated a moment, wondering how far into this he wanted to get. "What are you looking for? Fast growing, flowering?"

"I want something pretty that will last. It doesn't have to grow fast."

He pointed. "That tulip poplar over there will give you fantastic autumn foliage. Almost like aspens, which are related. It's pretty hardy, though."

She looked at the tree, which right now was little more than a twig with a few leaves. "Will it get really big?"

"It'll grow into a great shade tree."

That decided her. Ten minutes later he was carrying it out to his truck for her.

Holly felt as if someone had let all the air out of her. Grief? Maybe. More likely it was the release of the constant tension she lived with in Chicago. Fatigue seemed to envelop her, demanding she go home and fall asleep for hours, if not days. But she still had to plant a tree. She doubted that could be safely put off for too long.

"You ever planted a tree before?" Cliff's voice broke the silence she would have liked to continue forever.

"No."

There was a notable pause before he said, "I'll help."

His reluctance couldn't have been any more obvious. Hers equaled it. But before her pride could erupt and get her into trouble, she faced the fact that she needed the help. If she did it all wrong, she'd kill the tree. And from the size of the root ball, she questioned whether she'd even have the physical strength to dig a hole so big.

She glanced at Cliff from the corner of her eye. He'd have the strength. Damn it. "Thank you," she said quietly.

Another mile passed, then he surprised her by speaking again. "Your aunt was a remarkably caring, giving woman," he said. "If anyone in this county hit hard times, she was there for them. I guess you take after her."

Reluctantly, she looked at him. "How would you know?"

"I'm assuming. You're a social worker, right? That means you help people, right?"

She heard the annoyance in his tone and realized her response to him hadn't been very gracious. In fact, it had been challenging. Sheesh, she needed to get a handle on this antipathy toward him. He at least was making some kind of effort, much as she really didn't want it.

"In theory," she said. "Yeah, in theory. Once in a while I feel like I've gotten something good done. Most of the time I'm not sure. It takes kids a long time to grow up."

"You work with kids?"

"Mostly. With their parents, too, depending on what the problems are."

"Do you get any short-term rewards?"

The question surprised her with its understanding. She hadn't expected that. "Sometimes. But I'm not in it for rewards."

"No, you're in it to help."

The echo of her words a decade ago was so strong she winced. She distinctly remembered telling him that she had a bigger need to help people than she could meet around here as a rancher's wife. God, how full of herself she had been. She'd left wounds behind her as she'd set out like Don Quixote, with little idea of what she was getting into, or how many windmills would shatter her lance.

She didn't answer him, instead turning her attention to the countryside that rolled past. What was the point? They'd be better off having as little to do with each other as possible. It was just that simple. Hard to believe that a fleeting affair, however torrid, might have left scars that lingered this long.

She certainly hadn't expected it to.

One summer, a long, long time ago. She'd been visiting her aunt between semesters. He'd been gradually taking over the reins of his ranch from his father, just beginning to reach the fullness of manhood.

She had been sunning herself on a cheap, webbed chaise in the front yard, wearing a skimpy halter top and shorts, a book beside her on the grass. Martha had shooed her outdoors and was inside lining up a potluck dinner for her church. A potluck Holly had no intention of being dragged to. She was just a visitor, passing through, her sights set far away.

But then Cliff had come riding up. She hadn't seen his approach because he came from the rear of the house, but as he rounded the corner, she caught her breath. Against the brilliant blue clarity of the sky, he had looked iconic: astride a powerful horse, cowboy hat tipped low over a strong face, broad shouldered, powerful.

She should have run the instant she felt the irresistible pulse of desire within her. She should have headed for the hills. Instead, caught up in an instant spell, she had remained while his gaze swept over her, feeling almost like intimate fire, taking in her every curve and hollow. She'd felt desire before, but nothing like what this man had ignited within her.

Then the real folly had begun. She had to return to school in two months. She'd thought he understood that. When she talked about getting her master's and going into social work, she had thought her goals were clear. She had no intention of remaining in this out-of-the-way place as a rancher's wife, and just as she couldn't give up her dreams, he couldn't give up his ranch.

So who had been at fault, she wondered now, staring out the window. They had played with fire, they'd seized every opportunity to make love anywhere and everywhere, but then the idyll had come to an end. He had wanted her to stay.

She had snapped in some way. She had been living a fantasy of some kind, and he'd intruded on it with reality. She had thrown his declaration of love back in his face, then had called him stupid for thinking it could have ever been anything but a fling.

To this day she didn't know what had driven her cruelty. By nature she wasn't at all cruel, but that day... well, the memory of it still made her squirm. Maybe it had been a self-protective instinct, a way to end something that could move her life in a direction she didn't really want to go. Or maybe some part of her had been almost as desperate as he was, but in a different way.

She would probably never understand what she had done that day, but it had not only driven Cliff away, it had dashed the entire memory of that summer fling. She could not enjoy the memories of even the most beautiful or sexy moments of those weeks. All of it had to be consigned to some mental dustbin.

She had figured at the time that Martha must have known what was going on, but she'd never said a word. Now this? Maybe Martha hadn't guessed. If she had, then there was an unkindness here she wouldn't have believed her aunt capable of. And not just to her, but to Cliff, as well.

She sighed, pressing down memories that seemed to want to reignite right between her legs, reminding her of the dizzying pleasures she had shared with Cliff. That was gone, done for good. Over. Finished.

If only the words would settle it all in her body, which seemed inclined now to react as foolishly as it had all those years ago.

When he spoke, she felt so far away that his voice, deeper now than in the past, nearly startled her.

"I don't mean to sound like a rube," he said, then paused. "Hell, I *am* a rube. But I hear parts of Chicago can be pretty dangerous."

"They are," she said cautiously, wondering where he was headed.

"Did you work in those parts?"

"They're the parts where we're needed most, usually."

He fell silent, and she waited. Surely he wasn't going to leave it at that.

"You have guts," he said, and not one more word.

"No more than the people who have to live there."

"But you choose to be there, to help."

She couldn't imagine how to answer that. Yes, it was her choice, but the need cried out to her. She only wished she could provide a safer environment for those children, but the problems were huge. No one person could solve them.

"It's partly drugs," she said. "They encourage gang wars."

"Like during Prohibition."

"Yes, like that. Turf wars. Other things. Poverty grinds people down and sometimes brings out the ugliest parts of them. I just try to help kids so that they don't get drawn into it. There's not much else I can do to protect them, unless there's abuse in the family."

"It must feel thankless at times."

She couldn't believe he was talking to her in this sympathetic fashion. Not after the dislike that had radiated from him on their first meeting. Was he trying to mend bridges? She squirmed a little, thinking that if anyone should be trying to rebuild bridges, it was her. "Seeing just one kid make it is enough."

"Is it?"

She had no answer for that, either. But the tension that seemed to have lifted from her just by being away for a short while was settling heavily on her. She had matters to take care of here, she reminded herself. She had to decide what to do with her aunt's possessions, whether to rent the house—a million ends to tidy up. She couldn't spend all her time worrying about her kids back in Chicago, not when she was too far away to do anything.

Mercifully, he dropped the subject, and little by little, she returned fully to Conard County. She wished her kids could come out here, taste life without gunshots up the street any hour of the day or night and know what it was like to live even briefly without the fear.

She sighed, twisted her hands together and reset her sights on all that lay ahead of her.

What *was* she going to do with the house? Her job lay over a thousand miles away. She couldn't sell it. But renting it might lead to its ruination if she wasn't here to keep an eye on it.

Too soon, she argued with herself. She had time. No decisions had to be made this moment. Just plant the tree for Martha and then try to find comfort in residing in Martha's house, with all the good memories she had of her aunt.

She felt her eyes sting as she thought about Martha. The world had lost a true character and a great soul.

Cliff watched her from the corner of his eye, glancing her way from time to time as the road permitted. On a weekday, on these back roads, there wasn't a lot of traffic. Ahead of him stretched an empty road, its only danger the potholes left behind by winter. Along either side ran fences, often hidden behind the tumbleweeds caught in them, creating a low tunnel. But in those grasses to either side of the road, he knew there were drainage ditches, invisible in the grass, but enough to cause a minor accident.

So he really should keep his attention on driving. But just as she had done all those years ago, Holly drew him. The windows were open, thank goodness, otherwise he'd be assailed by her scents, and if there was one thing he knew for certain, he hadn't forgotten them. She still used the same shampoo; she still had the same enticing scent of femininity. Not strong, as it had been after they made love, but enough to remind him.

So here he was, stupidly walking into hell again. She'd only be here two weeks, long enough to get him all knotted up again, but completely lacking any kind of future. He hoped he had the sense to help her plant the tree and then go his way. Oh, he'd be a good neighbor and offer to keep an eye on the house when she left, but keeping an eye on a house wasn't anywhere nearly as dangerous as keeping an eye on Holly.

He wished her thinness, her evident fatigue, would turn him off. Instead, all it was doing was turning his insides into protective mush. He couldn't have this.

Inwardly he cussed himself for a fool, and warned himself to raise his guard. Do the minimum, stay away and turn his fullest attention to his own ranch, which had been all that had saved him all those years ago. Hard work was the answer.

Then she surprised him. She hadn't made a single friendly gesture, but now she did. Damn it.

"How's the ranch and business?"

Well, that ought to seem like a safe, casual question. Coming from her it felt freighted. "Okay," he said. Then realizing how abrupt he sounded, he added, "Leasing the acreage from your aunt has been a great help. It allowed me to expand."

"I heard cattle were getting more expensive to raise."

"Out of sight. We're transitioning to sheep. The wool market is still good."

"Good."

Clearly she wasn't really interested in his life. If he was honest, she hadn't been all that interested years ago, either. He might have found it easier to excuse her self-interest as youth if she hadn't followed it up with the coup de grâce.

Then, "Are sheep more difficult to raise?"

"Troubles come in all sizes and all degrees of fuzziness."

She surprised him with a laugh. "What a description!"

"It's true." He hated himself for wanting to smile. This was a demilitarized zone, not a party. "I traded one set of problems for another not so very different. The thing is, the sheep do better grazing on my land, and the wool comes every spring without me having to reduce my flock to make some money. Renewable resource."

"I like that."

He volunteered some more, testing her interest. "I also have a small herd of angora goats. They're a bit more susceptible to parasites, but their wool brings a higher price, so naturally it's more expensive to get going. Of course. So I'm growing my herd nature's way."

"It sounds like you have a plan."

"I hope so. Independent ranchers are in danger of becoming an extinct species. But I'm actually doing pretty well."

"I'm so glad to hear that, Cliff. So the sheep and goats get along well?"

"Well enough. My main headache is that the goats are more independent and adventurous. Keeping track of them can be a pain sometimes, and they need dietary additives. But when all is said and done, I like their antics."

Oh, well, he thought. He was going to have to deal with her at least some over the next couple of weeks. Greasing the skids with some superficial chitchat and courtesy ought to be safe enough. But no way was he going to fall into her honeyed web again.

Still, despite all the ugliness that had once happened, he couldn't help a twinge of concern. *Way too thin,* he thought as he glanced at her again. The bones in her face had become prominent, and her skin appeared stretched tightly across them. Not good.

But he didn't know how to ask without crossing into territory where she didn't want him to walk. Of that he was certain. He had begun to suspect that the past was no more buried for her than it was for him. Some things, it seemed, hurt forever.

He sought something else to say, and the question came out without thinking. "You married? Kids?"

"No and no."

It was a short answer, making it clear there were indeed limits to how personal she wanted to get with him. Hell, he thought, who was it who had taken out the scythe at their last meeting? Certainly not him.

"I tried it," he said finally, and waited.

Presently she asked, "And?"

"And it stank. Big-time. We couldn't shake the bottle hard enough to mix the oil and vinegar."

He waited, then heard a smothered laugh escape her. "I'm sorry, I shouldn't laugh, but your description…"

In spite of himself, he laughed, too. "Well, I can't think of a better one. Martha warned me."

"Really?"

He sensed her turn toward him for the first time. "Yeah. She said… Well, she was Martha. She asked me which head I was thinking with, and said that it would make more sense to ride my horse off a cliff than marry that woman. She was right."

"What happened?"

"Let's just say I went off the deep end for one woman and woke up to find myself married to a different one."

"Ouch."

"My ego needed some bandaging, but that was about it. Sometimes it just isn't meant to be."

She fell silent, and he let the subject go. It hadn't been right with Lisa, and chances were it wouldn't have been right with Holly, either. Not back then, for sure. Time to man up and admit it. He and Holly had been horses pulling in different directions, and if he'd been older and wiser he would have recognized it.

Well, he had learned his lessons. He hoped. All he needed to do was get that tree planted, see if Holly needed any other assistance and go back to his ranch, his sheep and his goats. It would take a special woman to want a life like that, and he couldn't afford to forget it.

They finally jolted up to Martha's house. "I need to get this road graded," he remarked. "It always goes to hell over the winter and spring, and that little car of yours is going to bounce like a Ping-Pong ball."

She didn't say anything, and he wondered if he'd trespassed by taking possession of the problem. He didn't know whether to sigh or roll his eyes. Oh, this was going to be fun. *Thank you very much, Martha.*

He braked without turning off the engine. "Where do you want to plant it?"

"I honestly don't know. I don't know how big it's going to get, how much sun it needs." She screwed up her face in the way he had once loved. "City girl here."

How could he forget that?

"Southwest corner," he suggested. "It'll get enough sun, keep the house cooler in the summer and lose all its leaves so it won't keep you colder in the winter."

"Sounds good to me."

Slowly he rolled the truck around the house. "It's going to need a lot of water the first month. And that's going to be a drag. Martha doesn't have an outside tap, so no hose."

"Really? I never noticed that before."

Why would she? She'd never been here long enough to really learn anything, although she had been here long enough to cause him a peck of trouble.

"I'll have someone see to it after you go home." That's as far as he would go. Or so he told himself.

"Thank you."

Damn it, he could almost hear Martha laughing and asking, "When did you turn into a chicken, boy?"

Then Holly said, "Martha always had such a big vegetable garden. She had to water it somehow."

"That's where the hand pump comes in. Come on, you were here lots of times. Surely you saw."

She paused. "My God, I'd forgotten. Of course I remember. I used to love to do it for her."

"Right. She planted in rows and pumped until the water filled the space between them. Every couple of days. The last few years it got harder for her, so I put in a motorized pump for her. Maybe you missed it."

"I guess so. My job gives me only short vacations."

"Well, it won't help with the tree regardless. It's going to be buckets."

"I can do that," she said stoutly.

He had his doubts, but maybe she was stronger than she looked right now.

The truth was, and he readily admitted it, he couldn't imagine her life in Chicago, nor how she could want to go back to it. Gunshots on the streets? The crushing poverty? Gang culture? Like so many, he had only a vague idea of how some people had to live. She volunteered to face that every day. From his point of view, it had certainly taken a toll on her.

Even so, when she walked ahead of him to pick out the exact spot for the tree, he couldn't help noticing the way her hips swayed. Or that when she turned her breasts were still full. A beautiful woman. A desirable woman.

Too bad.

When she'd chosen a spot, he headed for Martha's shed to get a shovel. While he did that, Holly disappeared inside, then returned with two tall glasses of iced tea.

"I seem to remember you liked sugar," she said, handing him one.

"Still do," he admitted. "I know it's a vice, but I work it off."

The corners of her mouth edged up a bit. "I guess you do. I can help with this."

"I don't know if you've ever tried to dig this ground around here, but we're going to be lucky if we don't need a backhoe."

That drew another small laugh from her. Angling the spade, he stood on it with one foot and penetrated the ground by about six inches. Good, the spring rains hadn't completely dried up yet. Dirt instead of concrete.

"Being in the house is difficult," Holly said quietly.

He looked up after tossing another shovelful of dirt to the side. "It is?"

"I keep expecting to hear Martha. To see her come around a corner. Even when it was just her and me, it never, ever seemed so silent in there."

He hadn't thought about that. He paused and looked back at the two-story clapboard house. "Yeah," he said finally. "I guess it would be quiet."

His gaze returned to Holly and he saw a tear rolling down her cheek. Whatever else he thought of her, he'd never doubted that she loved her aunt.

But talk about putting a man in an impossible bind. The thing to do would have been to hug her and comfort her. With anyone else, that's exactly what he would have done. But Holly was so far off-limits he couldn't even offer the most common act of sympathy. Finally he asked, "Are you going to be okay?"

She dashed the tear away. "Eventually. I just miss her so much. Damn, Cliff, I can't even call her anymore.

That keeps striking me over and over. I'll never hear her voice again."

He deepened and widened the hole with a few more spadefuls, then leaned on the handle and glanced at her.

"You can hear her voice," he said. "She's in your mind and heart now. Just give in to it and listen. If I know Martha, she's probably whispering something outrageous in your ear right this instant."

He finally got the hole big enough and put the tree in it. Kneeling, he tested the soil near the bottom and found it still held some moisture.

"Get a bucket of water," he told Holly. "Just flip the switch on the side of the pump and it'll start coming. There's a bucket in the shed."

She hopped to obey. It occurred to him he might have to prime the pump, so he was checking it out as she returned.

"Okay, it's ready. Put the bucket under the spout, hook it here." Like all good pumps, it had a nipple to hold a bucket handle. He showed her how to turn it on, then waited with her while it filled.

"There you go."

To his surprise, she lifted the five-gallon bucket and with both hands carried it over to the tree. Layer by layer, they watered lightly and refilled the hole. When he was done, he ridged the dirt in a ring around the tree. "Now fill this ring and just let it soak in. You'll probably need to do that every day."

He pulled off his work gloves, leaving her to it, and put the spade away. When he returned from the shed, he found her standing with an empty bucket, staring into space.

"Is something wrong?" he asked.

"It's just so peaceful out here. I wish some of my

kids could experience life like this, even if only for a short time."

Then he said the stupidest, most idiotic words to ever cross his lips. "So why don't you bring some of them out here?"

She looked at him then. *Really* looked at him, her blue eyes wide and almost wondering. His groin throbbed a warning. Had he really just suggested she come back here?

Man, he needed to finish up and get out of here *now*.

Chapter Three

Cliff left shortly after the tree was properly planted and watered. He'd even staked the slender trunk with bands in three directions so the wind wouldn't tip it over, or make it grow crooked, at least for now.

But then he was gone, and empty prairie winds blew around her. She stood looking toward the mountains, still dark green and gray in the early-afternoon sunlight, but soon the sun would sink behind them and the light would paint them purple.

She couldn't remember ever having felt so alone. Well, except for one night in Chicago, on a dark street when she had been attacked. She had felt alone in the world then, and it had seemed like forever before the cops had arrived. Someone in the poverty-stricken area had taken a huge risk calling them. She never knew who, and she didn't want to because she feared for the caller.

She had mostly gotten used to the conditions she worked in. When she wasn't making home visits, she was working with various programs designed to keep youngsters busy and off the streets. She was used to hearing random gunfire, though, used to the screeching of tires as some gang blew by, showing off their disdain for traffic laws and any unfortunate person who might be trying to cross a street.

Never alone, whether surrounded by good people or troublemakers. Except that one night. And now.

After the attack, she'd been given a few weeks off and had come here to recover. The contrast had really struck her then, and it was striking her now.

Except this time Martha wasn't here to listen, to advise, to sympathize. Another thing struck her right then: for all the tea, sympathy and advice, Martha hadn't even hinted that she should find a safer job. Not once.

She lifted her eyes to the sky and asked, "What's it all mean?"

Of course there was no answer. She turned from the tree and stared at the house. She could stay here. Martha had left her more than enough money that if she was careful she needn't ever work again.

But that didn't seem like something Martha would want for her, a dead-end existence without purpose. Martha had always been doing something for someone. A giver by nature.

And a great example.

So why don't you bring some of them out here? Cliff's question came back to her. Why not? She could imagine the red tape. Taking kids across state lines to spend a few weeks with her here? Not likely.

It was all too easy to imagine the hoops, then the structure she'd have to build. She couldn't do it alone.

She'd need help with the kids, trained help. She'd need things for them to do. Would they stay in the house or should she build a bunkhouse?

The next thing she knew, she was sitting in Martha's rocker on the front porch, rocking steadily, staring out over wide-open spaces, feeling an oddly healing touch in the emptiness of the world around here.

Those kids deserved a taste of this, she thought. An opportunity to live for a short while without the hunger and fear that filled their lives. To be able to fall asleep at night to quiet instead of gunshots.

She tried to dismiss the idea as utterly impractical. The amount of work in just getting it rolling, all the obstacles and roadblocks she'd run into. And while she was working on that, how could she keep up with her job?

Nor did she want to be so close to Cliff. He'd been pleasant enough today, she gave him credit for that, but her tension around him was almost as bad as her tension on a dark city street. It was an incautious, overwhelming desire for him, every bit as strong as it had been all those years ago when she'd given in to it and caused some serious pain.

And while she had never let Cliff know, leaving him behind hadn't been easy for her, either. No, she hadn't wanted the commitment he was offering. Hadn't been ready for it. Had been set on her goal to help kids to the point that she couldn't imagine any other life.

So she had gotten what she really wanted, and now life had brought her full circle to deal with all the unanswered questions.

How could she best help those kids? And why did she still want Cliff?

Why don't you just bring some of them out here?

Why had he asked that question? What had he been thinking? His face had revealed nothing, but he'd been quick to leave after that, as quick as he could.

Could she stand being this close to him for any length of time, which bringing kids out here would require? But as soon as she asked herself, she felt selfish. If there was some way to help kids with her legacy, then she needed to do it, Cliff or no Cliff.

But maybe bringing those kids out here for even a few weeks or months might not be kind at all. To give them a taste of a different life and then plop them back into their old messes? It would help only if she could make them see possibilities to work for when they got home. Dreams they could believe in.

Propping her chin in her hand, unaware that the afternoon was fading into twilight, she twisted the idea around in her head, half wishing Cliff had never mentioned it, half wishing she could find a useful way to do it.

The chill of the night penetrated finally, and she went inside to make herself a small supper. Once again the empty silence of the house hit her hard, making her eyes sting and her chest tighten.

Live here alone forever? No way. Somehow there had to be another way. A better way. A useful way.

Damn memory, Cliff thought. He'd given up all hope of sleeping. Again. Since he'd heard that he was going to have to see Holly again, he'd been an insomniac, and now the insomnia had grown to devour most of the night hours.

As for memory...there were all kinds of it, he was discovering. He wasn't remembering the way Holly had looked all those years ago. No. Mental pictures had nothing to do with it.

Instead his mind was plaguing him with the sounds she made during passionate sex. His hands, indeed his entire body, were resurrecting the way her skin had felt against him, the way she felt beneath him. His palms itched with the certain knowledge of how it felt to caress her, how her breasts felt in his hands, the hard way her nipples pebbled, the dewiness of her womanhood.

And scents. They filled his nostrils almost as if she were right there, sated and content.

He even remembered exactly, *exactly,* how it had felt to plunge into her warm depths.

Much as he tried to banish the thoughts, they planted themselves and stayed like unfinished business. He couldn't see Martha's house from his place, but it didn't matter. There weren't enough hundreds of square miles in this county to make him comfortable when she was in it.

His body ached with a need to take her again, to touch her again, to fill her again. Not even his wife had ever awakened such a craving in him.

Damn Holly, damn Martha and, God, he hoped that she didn't take that stupid thought of his seriously. Bring those kids here? He couldn't imagine the scope of the undertaking, but even less could he imagine life with Holly nearby. This county wasn't big enough for both of them.

He shoved out of his bed impatiently, aware that if he didn't watch it he was going to make love to Holly in his mind. Maybe that had been part of the problem in his marriage with Lisa. Maybe at some unconscious level he had considered Lisa second best.

He didn't know, but if so, he ought to despise himself. Staring out the window at a night as dark as pitch, he wrestled his internal demons.

Ten years later, even after the awful way she had treated him, he still wanted her as much as the very first time. Did that make him sick? He didn't know that, either.

He just knew that seeing her had fueled a fire that had never quite gone out. Now what the hell was he going to do about it?

He'd thought he'd finally learned to roll with life, the good and the bad, but now he wondered. That woman out there had the ability to turn him into a kid again. He was randier than a goat, and it didn't please him.

Sometimes, on rare, restless nights, he'd go saddle up Sy and take a ride. The gelding seemed to enjoy those nighttime rambles. He let Sy choose the course and the pace, and sometimes that gelding would open up his throttle wide and gallop hell-for-leather.

But it was a moonless, dark night, not safe for riding, and besides, he had a feeling that if he mounted up, he'd end up at Martha's place like a lovesick dog.

So he stood there aching, remembering, knowing it had been a dream that could never happen again. He needed to get a grip.

But the grip kept slipping away, lost in dizzying sensual memories.

A few miles away, Holly wasn't doing much better. She had fallen asleep only to wake twisted in her sheets and drenched in perspiration. She had dreamed of Cliff, which she hadn't done in years, but it had gotten all twisted up in her dream with the guys who had attacked her last year.

How could she want something that still frightened her? That overlayering of the attack ought to be a warning. She'd avoided dating since then, because she couldn't quite erase the memory of stinking breath and pawing, filthy hands. Any time a guy got too close, she headed for the door.

But she'd done the same to Cliff before then, and for the first time she wondered who she really was and what might be going on inside her.

All she knew was that Cliff still drew her as he had from the first. At least the years had made her considerably less self-centered. She'd hurt the man badly, and she wasn't going to risk doing it again, whether she craved him or not.

She just wished she knew what it was about him. Nobody had ever gotten to her the way he had.

She took the teddy bear from the chair and pulled it over to the window. Even with the curtains open, she couldn't see much, but she didn't care. She lifted the sash just a bit, letting some chilly air into the room, hoping it would cool her down. Then she hugged the bear and sat, watching the impenetrable night.

Thinking about Cliff was the ultimate waste of time, she told herself. She'd hurt him badly, and while he'd been civil and even pleasant today, that had been common courtesy. It had been obvious to her at their first meeting that he ranked her somewhere near rat poison on his list of things he liked. Nor could she blame him. She had burned that bridge herself.

She tried instead to think about the little kernels of an idea he had planted today, but her mind remained stubborn. Even as her body dried off and began to feel chilled, Cliff persisted in dominating her thoughts.

A decade had passed and she still wanted him. That was surely crazy.

Then she saw movement outside. She leaned toward the window and strained her eyes. Horse and rider? *What the*— Jumping up, she pulled off her damp nightgown, pulled on a dry and much more modest one, then headed downstairs.

She was sure of one thing: only one person would be riding up to this house in the middle of the night.

She reached the front door just as he came riding around the corner of the house. He wasn't even looking in her direction, just kind of ambling along. She grabbed a jacket off the coat tree, pulled it on and stepped out.

"What are you doing?" she asked.

He drew rein and turned his mount in her direction. "Curing insomnia," he said. "We shouldn't have disturbed you."

"You didn't. I was awake."

"Sorry I didn't bring a horse for you."

Oh, that was a mistake, she thought as memory slammed her again. They'd gone riding together so many times during that summer, laughing and carefree until passion would rise again. They'd made love on a bed of pine needles, once on a flat rock in the middle of a tumbling mountain stream, another time…

Clenching her hands, she forced memory back into its cage. "Does it help the insomnia? Riding?" It seemed like a safe question.

"I don't think anything's going to help tonight," he said bluntly.

Even though she could barely see him, she could feel his eyes boring into her. The quiet night settled between them, disturbed only by the jingle of the horse's bridle as it tossed its head a little.

"Well," he said, "we'll just move on."

She knew what she should have done, but before

she could act sensibly, words popped out of her mouth. "Want some coffee? I know it won't help you sleep…"

"It's almost dawn. No point in sleeping now." For a few seconds it seemed he was going to continue his ride, but then he swung down from the saddle. "Coffee would be great."

She turned quickly and headed back inside, partly to avoid getting too close to him, and partly to warm up. Late spring? The nights still got chilly.

She wished she'd grabbed a robe, but the long flannel nightgown she had put on was probably almost as concealing. Which led her to another question as she made the coffee. Why had she been in such a rush to get down here when she had been certain it was Cliff riding by?

She shook her head at her own behavior. Maybe this house just felt too empty with Martha, but it was pretty sad that she was reaching out to Cliff.

So there she was, missing Martha even more because she ought to be here, hundreds of miles from home, troubled by a weird nightmare that had somehow combined Cliff with the attack on her when the two were totally unrelated. She wondered if she was losing it.

Or maybe grief had just scrambled her thinking. It was certainly possible.

She heard Cliff come through the house to the kitchen, and it seemed his steps were slow. Evidently he wasn't really looking forward to having coffee with her. Well, why should he? But he could have just refused.

"Have a seat," she said. She remained where she was, staring at a coffeemaker that seemed to be taking forever and a window that stared back at her blackly, showing her more of the kitchen behind her than the world outside.

It was a big country kitchen. Martha had once talked

about the days when the family was big, when they had hired help and everyone would gather here for the main meal of the day. At home she had an efficiency, with barely enough room for a narrow stove, small sink and tiny refrigerator. If she wanted to cook, she had to do the prep on her dining table in the next tiny room.

Still, the house was awfully big for one person, but she couldn't sell it for ten years. She definitely needed to find a good way to put it to use.

Wandering thoughts again, but when the coffeemaker finished, so did the wandering.

"You still like it black?" she asked.

"Yes. Thanks."

So she carried two mugs to the table, and finally had to sit facing him. No way to avoid it any longer.

He looked tired, she thought. Well, lack of sleep would do that. But damn him, he remained every bit as sexy as he had all those years ago. Maybe even more so. That didn't seem fair.

"You've lost weight," he remarked. "Have you been sick?"

She shook her head. "Just busy. Sometimes I just feel too tired to eat."

"That's not good." When she didn't answer, he spoke again. "I take it your job is draining. Want to tell me about it?"

"What's to tell? I work with people most of society doesn't care about. People who never had a real chance in life. Most of my job is trying to get children to do the things that will give them a chance. To avoid the things that will take away their chances. We try to give them a safe environment after school, encourage them to fin-ish homework, feed them, expand their horizons a bit. And then they go home to the same despair."

He gave a low whistle.

"Maybe that's not entirely fair," she said after a moment. "There are some bad parents. There are in any group. When I first started I was investigating abuse cases that occurred at very nice addresses. Then I moved over to work with underprivileged kids. A lot of people may not believe it, but some of my strongest supporters with these kids are their parents. They want their children to have a better life. But it's kind of hard to believe in when you come home to a run-down apartment where no one cares enough even to get rid of the roaches, and there's little food in the refrigerator."

"Colliding worlds?"

She nodded, closing her eyes. "You have to take it a step at a time," she said finally. "Right now I'm organizing a couple of communities to demand exterminators. You'd think management would at least provide that. Little kids shouldn't be living with roaches, rats and mice. It's not healthy. Sometimes they get bitten."

"God!"

"Anyway, sometimes I feel like I'm trying to hold back a flood with a broom. These people are so ground down. But then you see the spark of hope in them when they think you can help their kids. They really care about that."

"But you're just one person."

"But I'm not the only social worker. We do what we can. It's hard not to get impatient, though. I could use a magic wand."

"I imagine so."

She opened her eyes, but looked back toward the window. "What you said earlier about bringing some of them out here?"

She noticed his response was hesitant. "Yeah?"

"I wish I could. I was thinking about it, but the problems are huge. And while Martha might approve, I'd need to get through all kinds of red tape. And then I asked myself what I could do for them in a couple of weeks here. Or even a whole summer here. Would I just make it harder on them when they had to go home?"

"That's a tough question. I didn't think about that."

She shrugged and finally managed to look at him again. "It needs a lot of planning in a lot of ways. But I keep thinking how wonderful it might be for them to have a month or two when they just simply didn't have to be afraid or hungry."

"So they're afraid, too?"

"They're living in a damn war zone. Gangs. Drugs. Turf wars. They learn to be afraid very early."

He cursed. "That's no way for a kid to grow up."

"I agree. But as one of my friends often reminds me, a lot of kids in the world are growing up exactly that way."

"But it ought to be different in *this* country."

He spoke with so much vehemence that she blinked. She'd never had time before to find out if Cliff had a social conscience. Apparently he did.

She glanced away toward the window again. She didn't want to find any reasons to like this guy. None. She'd be leaving again in two weeks, whatever she decided to do with this ranch.

But then her thoughts wandered a different, faraway path. "You get used to it," she said presently. "You just get used to it."

"Have you?"

"I guess so. I didn't realize until I got here just how much tension I was carrying all the time. My first night here I could feel it letting go. Something inside me is uncoiling. But it never uncoils for those children. Even in a safe place, like their homes, or at the youth center, I'm sure it never has long enough to let go because in just a short while they're going to step outside again."

He didn't offer any bromides, but she heard him drum his fingers on the table. She needed to get away from this subject for a little while, she realized, because even just talking about it and thinking about it was ratcheting up her tension.

She fixed him with her gaze. "Do you have a lot of insomnia?"

"Sometimes. Usually not this bad."

"I'd think with how hard you work, you'd just conk out."

"You'd think." He gave her a crooked smile. "Maybe I'm just one of those people who doesn't need a whole lot of sleep. I certainly don't walk around feeling sleep deprived."

"I can't imagine it. Sometimes I think I could sleep around the clock."

"Maybe I should let you get back to it."

The perfect out. She should have grabbed it, but she didn't. "No, I'm fine. I think I'm done with sleep tonight. I was sitting upstairs thinking about things when I saw you ride up. I'm wondering if this house is always going to feel so achingly empty without Martha."

"I don't know. I wish I could tell you. I miss her, too, and I didn't even live here, but you're right, I keep expecting to hear her voice."

"Yeah. And for some reason I'm focusing on that. That I'll never hear her voice again except inside my own head."

He hesitated visibly, then said, "Martha told me you were attacked once in Chicago."

At that instant she seriously wanted to throw him
out. His company had at least distracted her from that
mixed-up dream where one instant she was with Cliff
in the throes of passion and in the next she was being
grabbed and pawed by that slimeball. She still didn't
understand why her mind had hooked those two things
together, even in a dream, but she certainly didn't want
to think about the attack.

He must have read her face. "Sorry. I shouldn't have
brought that up, but I've worried about you ever since."

"Why should you worry at all about me after the
way I treated you?" she demanded, angry but not at all
sure whether she was mad at him or something else.
"And that was *my* business. Why would Martha tell
you about that?"

He responded to her anger, his face darkening. "She
worried about you. Constantly. Maybe she never told
you, but she did. And after that, I worried, too. There's
a lot of crap between us, Holly. I've got plenty of reason not to like you. But that doesn't mean I don't care
what happens to you."

He pushed back from the table. His face had grown
hard, and his voice chilly. "Call me if you need anything. Martha put me on autodial."

Then he walked out. Just like that. Not even a goodbye.

She sat alone at the table, cooling coffee in front of
her, trying to sort through the tangled web of emotions
inside her, but it proved impossible. All of it was impossible. She couldn't imagine how she would ever get
herself straightened out.

Coming back here had been a mistake. Dealing with
rough neighborhoods by and large wasn't nearly as dangerous as dealing with emotions. Things that could kill

your body weren't half as scary as things that could kill your heart.

Then she put her head down on the table and let the tears roll. Martha. Cliff. The past. The present. The only thing she was certain of was that she missed Martha with a grinding ache.

And sometimes, like now, her brain would furtively sneak in a question she didn't want to hear: Had she made a mistake by not staying here and marrying Cliff?

Too late now, but apparently part of her would always wonder.

Damn, when she had raced to get out here, she had assumed that she wouldn't see Cliff. He'd steadfastly stayed away during her visits to Martha after their affair, and it hadn't crossed her mind that it would be different this time.

But here she was, and Cliff wasn't staying away. Not at all. Although if she was to judge by the way he had just left, he might not come back.

That would be for the best, she told herself. Much better if she never laid eyes on him again. Even after all these years, he could still roil her emotions and waken her passions, and she really didn't need that. Not now, not ever.

Cliff steamed as he rode home, but he reserved his anger for himself. He'd been stupid to accept Holly's offer of coffee. He knew that woman could sting him, but he'd put himself right in the line of fire. Nobody to blame but himself.

As for her being upset that he knew she had been attacked, what was that? It hardly amounted to a shameful secret, and both he and Martha had worried about her. Hell, Martha had often talked about Holly and her concerns. Who else was she going to talk to? Nobody else around here knew Holly.

At first he'd found it uncomfortable to talk about the woman who had torched his hopes, but time had made it easier. He wondered about Martha, though, and about this whole setup.

Martha was no fool. She must have guessed what was going on between him and Holly that long-ago summer. At their age, she'd probably guessed they weren't just two friends who liked to spend long hours alone with each other. No, she had to have known, even though she'd never said a word.

Of course, she couldn't have known why they broke up. Maybe she thought it had been reasonably friendly. That much was possible, and might explain the current insanity of his being executor of the estate.

But why tell Holly she couldn't sell the house for ten years? And while being executor didn't exactly burden him with things he *had* to do, it remained that he felt Martha had meant him to keep an eye on things. Keep an eye on Holly.

Hell.

He almost muttered under his breath. Sy was getting a little antsy, though, probably picking up on his mood. The light wasn't so great yet, although the first signs of dawn rode the eastern horizon. Regardless, he slackened the reins, trusting Sy to choose his own pace and safe ground. He'd long since learned it was the safest way to let a horse open up. They seemed to smell prairie-dog holes well in advance, and tc see other obstacles quickly.

With the lack of tension, Sy cut loose. He hit a full gallop across the rangeland, maybe half a mile, then settled into a comfortable walk again. Cliff leaned forward, patting his neck.

"Better, boy?"

Sy tossed his head.

"I guess so." But it wasn't better for Cliff. He hadn't been the one galloping. The question remained: What had Martha expected of him? And if she'd expected something, why hadn't she given him a clue? Apparently, she hadn't given Holly any clues, either, except that stuff about finding her dream. That was certainly opaque.

He sighed, feeling the last of the night's chilly air, and tried to corral his thoughts. He had a lot to do today, and no energy to waste on thinking about Holly. He'd deal with whatever turned up as it became necessary.

In theory she was going back to Chicago in just under two weeks. Back to the job she had always wanted. A job that he thought might be slowly killing her. But what did he know?

He rode around to the barn and turned Sy over to one of his hired hands. He usually cared for the horse himself, but this morning he didn't feel like it.

Ruben took the reins from him. "You got company, Boss."

"What kind?"

"The kind that comes in a sports car."

"Out here?" Cliff's brows raised. He tried to think of anyone who might have business with him, because his neighbors and friends sure didn't drive those cars. Useless out here.

He walked in through the back door and mudroom. His housekeeper, Jean, was at the kitchen sink. She looked at him, and her expression held none of its usual welcome.

"She's in the living room."

"Who?"

"Go look."

He shook his head, wondering what the hell was going on. "Coffee?"

"Grab some."

So he did, then headed for whatever was awaiting him. He reached the threshold of the living room and froze. "Lisa?" he asked with disbelief.

His former wife was stretched out on the sofa as if posed for a photo, showing her cleavage to best advantage, her long black hair draped perfectly as if to draw attention to her most notable feature.

The only good thing he could say about her arrival was that he felt no response whatever to her blatant sexuality. At least that part was dead for good. But his dislike of her lived on. He wanted to roar at her to get out of his house.

"Hi, Cliff," she said, her voice sultry. "I've been thinking a lot about you and missing you. You don't mind, do you?"

Did he mind? Hell, yeah. He was already trying to figure out ways to make her leave. But he needed a minute to put a lid on his temper, too. She couldn't have called to ask first? "I've gotta get some breakfast. You wait here."

In the kitchen, Jean simply frowned at him.

"You should have sent her away," he said.

"Not my place. But if she stays, I go."

Back to that. Lisa had almost cost him Jean six years ago, and Jean was part of the family—she'd been here his entire life. "She's not staying."

"Ha!"

"I mean it."

"She already brought in her suitcases."

"Then I'll take them out."

"Good luck."

He opened a cupboard. "Breakfast?"

"Find your own. I'm not cooking for that woman."

Cliff closed his eyes for a moment, wondering if life could get any more complicated. Well, of course it could. Lisa was here.

He settled for a bowl of cold cereal and headed back to the living room. He took the chair farthest from Lisa.

"So what's going on?" he asked bluntly.

"I told you. I missed you."

"You haven't missed me in six years."

She pouted. "That's not true."

"Just spit it out, Lisa. Spare me the drama."

"Oh, all right then," she said, sitting up, but leaning forward so her cleavage remained on display. He wondered why he had ever found that attractive. Right now he felt repelled.

"I'm between jobs," she said.

"Really? Between marriages, too, I guess." He knew she had married some guy up near Gillette, because once she had he'd no longer owed her alimony.

"Well, yes."

"Sorry. What am I supposed to do about any of this?"

"Like I said, I'm between jobs. I just need a few weeks."

"A few weeks?" His entire household would fall apart, and even some of his hired hands might desert him in that time. Lisa was nothing if not imperious.

"Yes."

"And how are you going to find a job out here?"

She frowned. "I already have a job. Damn it, Cliff,

don't be a jerk. I start my new job in two weeks. I just need a place to stay until then."

He was finding this hard to believe. Something about this smelled to high heaven. "What else aren't you telling me?"

"Nothing." Her dark eyes flashed. "You're still a jerk, aren't you."

"I don't like being lied to."

"Well, I'm not lying. I have a job in Glenwood Springs, but I have no way of getting a place to stay until then. If I spend money renting a place now, I won't make it until I get my first paycheck. That is all there is to it."

It was almost believable. Maybe it was even the truth. But he sat there wondering whether she really wanted to stay here for two weeks, or if she wanted him to front her some money. Either one looked impossible right now. It was late spring, he hadn't yet gotten the money for his wool, he had vet bills, especially for the new lambs and kids, he needed to… Well, he just wasn't flush at the moment.

He looked at his bowl of cereal and realized that while he might need to eat, he couldn't swallow a thing right now.

"I want you out of here," he said flatly. "Try your sob story on someone else. Jean is already threatening to leave."

"Jean always mattered more than I did," she pouted.

"Unfortunately, I made the mistake of letting you matter more once upon a time. I lost three good hands because of you, and barely kept Jean. You have no idea of the havoc you managed to wreak and how long it took me to put things back together. I'm not doing that again."

She stood up. "When did you become so cruel? I have nowhere to go!"

He felt a twinge of conscience, but tried to quash it. If this woman weren't poison, he'd give her the two weeks. But he'd learned his lesson the hard way.

Without a word, he got up and went back to the kitchen. Jean was sitting at the table at a time of day when she would ordinarily have been working on something for the midday's big meal for him and his hands. He dumped the cereal, rinsed the bowl and sat facing Jean.

"She says she has nowhere to go."

Jean scowled.

"For two weeks."

Jean's frown deepened. "Do you really believe her?"

"Damned if I know. The thing is…"

"The thing is, you've always been too generous for your own good." Since Jean had helped raise him, he was used to her having her say. "You don't want her here. I don't want her here. She's a troublemaker."

"But if she's not lying…"

Jean sighed. "If she's not lying, then whose fault is it she has no one to turn to but you?"

Hard to argue with that. But despite his anger that she was here, he couldn't exactly kick her to the curb. "Can you handle it for a few days?"

Jean rolled her eyes. "I knew it. I knew it the minute she marched into this house right past me with a suitcase. As if she owns the place even now."

"I know what she's like. I'm asking *you*."

"I put up with her for two years for your sake. I suppose I can manage a few days. But I warn you, I'm not going to bite my tongue this time. Not like I did before."

"It's better for you if you don't. I'm going to figure out a way to get her out of here as quickly as possible."

Jean just shook her head. "When did you ever get that woman to do what *you* wanted?"

Good question, he thought as he marched back into the living room. Lisa had given up on the sultry pose, exchanging it for one that looked like avenging fury. As if she had a right. But Lisa had never needed anyone else to grant her a right. She took them all as she chose.

"You can stay here a couple of days until you find something else. That's it. And be forewarned, I don't want Jean or anyone else upset. Period."

He watched Lisa struggle to find a grateful smile. She almost made it. "Thank you."

He grabbed a couple of bananas and headed out to work. All of a sudden it seemed the world was determined to turn upside down.

Oh, to hell with it. They could endure anything for a couple of days, even Lisa.

Chapter Four

Holly had spent the day puttering around, getting used to the silent house, deciding which things she should keep and which should go. Martha's clothes needed to be donated, but beyond that she found decisions remarkably hard. She did find a small stack of bills in Martha's desk, unopened, so she pulled out her new checkbook and paid them. She supposed she needed to have the utilities and so on put in her name. She wondered if she would need Cliff for that.

She didn't especially feel like seeing him again, even if her thoughts kept wandering his way. She wished she could just understand why she felt so attracted to him. That should have faded, shouldn't it?

Apparently not.

On and off, though, she remembered his remark about bringing some of her kids out here. During the late afternoon, she went outside to water the tree and walked around, thinking of what she might be able to do on the land that hadn't been fenced. There was a surprising amount of space. Martha's big vegetable garden, now mostly a memory under a layer of grass and weeds, was still there. There was room to build some kind of bunkhouse, maybe two, where the kids could stay, either with their families or with counselors, depending. There was even enough room to make a pen for a few goats or sheep for them to work with.

She stood there for a long time, envisioning, still wondering if it would be good or bad to take these kids into a whole different world for a few weeks or months. She ought to call her friend who was a child psychologist and ask. Opening up possibilities seemed like a good idea overall. Sending them back home to a misery that might feel even worse once they knew it didn't have to be that way, not so good.

"Hello."

Startled by the voice, she pivoted to see a striking woman astride a horse at the fence line. She wondered if she had been so deeply lost in thought that she hadn't heard her approach or if the wind had whisked the sounds away.

Either way, it astonished her. Could she have relaxed so much here already that her situational awareness had dulled? She didn't like the way her stomach sank at the possibility that this was Cliff's current girlfriend. He hadn't mentioned one, but that didn't mean a damn thing.

"Hi," she said, managing a smile, trying to tell herself she didn't care. Her visitor was quite a beautiful woman, with inky hair and dark eyes. Exotic, even in jeans and a plaid shirt with rolled-up sleeves.

"I was looking for Martha," the woman said.

"I'm sorry, she passed away. I'm her niece, Holly.
Did you know Martha well?"

"I used to. I've been away. I'm Lisa. Cliff's ex-wife."

Talk about a bombshell. Holly didn't quite know how
to answer that. In fact she didn't know if she wanted to
say anything at all. Even less when she suddenly realized that this woman had totally skipped the usual and
conventional first response of "I'm sorry about Martha." She remained silent, waiting. Maybe she was being
rude, but something about this woman raised her hack-
les. She hoped it wasn't jealousy, because she certainly
had no reason to be jealous. The part she didn't want
to think about was the way her stomach had sunk. She
ignored it as best she could. She had no hopes here, no
reason to feel kicked by this news.

"So do you own the place now?" Lisa asked.

"Yes." Every instinct warned Holly that this conversation wasn't headed somewhere casual. It had a
direction.

Lisa smiled broadly. "I was coming to ask for Martha's help, but maybe you'll help me out instead."

Bingo, thought Holly. "How's that?"

"I need a place to stay for a few weeks. Cliff won't
let me stay for more than a couple of days."

Good heavens. The chutzpah! Asking her ex to take
her in, and then when he was reluctant she asked a total
stranger? Without even a brief expression of sympathy
for Martha's passing?

Holly felt as if she were looking at an alien. However, she wasn't prepared to be rude just yet. Maybe
this woman was in need? If so, she had to help. That
was a deeply ingrained part of her nature. "Are you
talking about renting a room?" That would be impossible, given that Holly had to go back to Chicago. She

didn't know that she wanted to turn this house over to a total stranger, certainly not when it was full of Martha's belongings.

Lisa looked woeful. "I wish I could. I'm between jobs and it's just awful that Cliff won't let me stay. I can't afford to rent a place. Am I supposed to live in my car?"

"A lot of people do," Holly couldn't help saying, and while those people didn't like it, almost none of them whined about it. They felt fortunate to have shelter better than a cardboard box. "I work with some of them."

"Then you know how awful it would be!"

Holly couldn't deny that. Especially for a woman alone. And, in spite of herself, she was getting interested. Regardless, she could either do the decent thing or feel guilty. It wouldn't be the first time she'd taken in a stranger, although when she did it in Chicago, it was usually a woman in much worse straits than this.

"I can offer you a room," she said finally. "But not for long. I'll be closing the place up in ten days because I have to get home."

"That would still be a great help! I'll get my things."

Holly watched her ride away, wondering what she had gotten herself into. But ten days? It was a short time and the company might be welcome. At least she wouldn't leave the woman to live in her car.

And at least she wouldn't be alone in the echoing silence.

"You did what?" Cliff demanded as he watched Lisa load her car. They stood outside in the driveway, near her red sports car as she put suitcases in her trunk. He didn't offer to help her.

"You didn't want me, but the woman who owns Martha's place now said I could stay with her until she has to go home." Lisa sniffed. "She's kinder to a stranger than you are to your ex-wife."

"There's a reason you're the ex." He swore.

"Well, you got what you wanted," Lisa said with a toss of her head. "I'll be out of your way, and your precious Jean won't be bothered."

He watched Lisa drive away, then hurried into the house to grab a phone. Holly answered on the second ring.

"You offered my ex a place to stay?"

"Well, why not? It's only a few days. Maybe I need the company."

"Not this company."

"Cliff, I understand she's your ex, but we're strangers. We don't have any problems between us."

"You will," he said grimly. "Jean nearly left me because of her. I had three hired hands quit because of her."

"Oh, she can't be that bad."

"Wanna bet? She's a princess in her own mind. I hope you're ready to take on cooking, cleaning and laundry for her."

"I just won't do it."

"Right. I'm coming over."

"You don't need to."

"Look, she's on her way. I'm coming over and you and I are going to have a talk about Lisa."

"Why?"

"Because I need to defend myself and maybe you." He hung up. Hell and damnation!

This was getting truly bizarre, Holly thought as she hung up the phone. If Lisa was homeless, even temporarily, then it was only right to help her out. Her conscience wouldn't allow otherwise. She could understand why Cliff wouldn't want his ex to stay with him. Regardless of what the woman was like, there was probably a lot of tension there. But what had he meant about his hired hands and Jean?

She guessed she was going to find out, just as she was going to find out why he needed to defend himself and possibly her.

Sheesh, she thought with amusement. He was making Lisa sound like the plague. Surely she couldn't be that bad. Insensitive, yes, that was already apparent, but short of thievery or murder, how bad could she be?

She went back inside to check Martha's room to make sure it was ready. Fresh sheets already graced the bed, but after a moment's hesitation she took Martha's jewelry box to her own room. Not that Martha had had any expensive jewelry, but Holly had liked some of it since childhood, like an enameled pin of a black cat with a rhinestone eye and gold collar. She didn't want to lose any of it until she'd had a chance to go through it.

Then she grabbed some bags and began to fill them with Martha's clothes. Sorting could wait, but for now she needed to make space for her guest. If guest she was.

She had just finished emptying the drawers and closet and dragging the bags to the top of the stairs when she heard a car pull in. That must be Lisa. Once more she wondered what she had gotten into, but decided yet again that it ought to be interesting, whatever it was. The distraction would be a good thing. Rattling around in this house, expecting Martha to come around a corner or out of a door, was just making her sadder. She needed to grieve, yes, but nothing said she had to do it in solitude and without interruption.

Besides, she was beginning to discover that time was hanging heavy on her hands. Deciding what to do about the house and its contents seemed almost beyond her right now, and she wasn't used to being alone all the time. She was used to having a job. Having friends. Needing solitude only after a truly trying day. Being alone too much was also allowing her mind to wander all kinds of paths, too many of which seemed to lead her right back to Cliff. Cliff, who should have just remained firmly in the past, but now was very much in the present.

Along with his ex-wife. She almost laughed at the total absurdity of all this.

She dragged the bags down the stairs, but before she reached bottom Lisa had opened the front door and walked in. No knock, no ring, no polite request to enter. Just Lisa and a suitcase.

Holly began to get an inkling of what this was going to be like. Maybe Cliff hadn't been exaggerating.

Nor did Lisa offer to help her with the bags of clothing. She just stepped to the side, set her suitcase down and said, "When you get done with that you can help me with my other things."

In a flash, Holly's dander rose. "I am not your maid. Get your own things. Top of the stairs, room on the right."

"That wasn't very courteous."

"Neither were you."

Wasting not another glance on the woman, Holly placed the bags by the back door. Just as she was considering what the heck she was going to do about dinner when all she had was one small chicken breast and some leftover salad, she heard another vehicle pull up. Cliff?

Leaving dinner for later consideration, she hurried to

the front. It was indeed Cliff and he was standing with Lisa beside her car, looking very stubborn.

She opened the door and stepped out in time to hear him say, "You never asked anyone if you could come here, you just showed up. Now you're imposing on my friend, who is in the process of grieving and trying to sort out her aunt's affairs, and the only thing that concerns you is whether I'll carry your suitcases?"

"It seems like the polite thing to do."

"When you learn some politeness, we'll talk about mine."

He turned from Lisa and saw Holly. "Let's take a walk, Holly."

"Now that really is rude," Lisa snapped. Then she, too, turned toward Holly. "Don't believe a word he says about me. Exes never have anything nice to say."

Holly kept silent while she and Cliff walked toward the fence, far enough from Lisa that they wouldn't be heard if they kept their voices low. Then she said, "I guess I really stepped into the middle of it."

"It's not your fault. She put you in the middle. I just wish I knew what her game is."

"Why does there have to be a game? Maybe she really does just need a place to stay for two weeks."

He leaned against a fence post and faced her. "Maybe. Not likely. Regardless, I know I look like a total boor refusing to carry her bags for her, but I am absolutely not going to help her move in on you. Maybe she'll get mad enough to find another place. I'm certainly going to try to find her one."

Holly hesitated. "Was she always this demanding?"

"It got worse with time."

"And Jean was really prepared to leave?"

"When the woman who helped raise you says, 'It's

her or me,' you listen. Which is not to say I divorced Lisa just over that. I'd been building up a head of steam in that direction for quite awhile." He paused, then gave a shake of his head. "I got so I couldn't stand her anymore. She was driving me and everyone else nuts in her own special way, but I'd taken a vow. Funny, but I take vows seriously. Even when keeping them is driving everyone away and nearly ruining my business."

"Wow! What in the world was she doing?"

"Like I said, driving people away. Spending as if money grew on trees." He shook his head again. "I finally got sick of getting to the bills, only to find that I needed my credit extended because there was nothing left. Or getting overdraft notices. So I gave her her own checking account and told her that was all she got for the month."

"How long did that work?"

"For about two weeks. Then the bank would be calling. Then she'd be whining or screaming. Honestly, Holly, if I'd had any inkling I'd never have married her."

Holly frowned, looking down at the ground and kicking at a tuft of wild grass. "Some of that is straight up abusive behavior. I've watched men cut their girlfriends and wives off from everyone until they hadn't a friend or family member left to turn to. I've seen men, and women, who'd spend all the money as soon as a spouse's paycheck arrived and leave nothing for food, nothing for the kids. It's common enough, sad to say."

"I guess. My friends started dropping away because Lisa was always there, then three of my hands quit because she treated them like her personal servants and was always asking them to do things they hadn't been hired to do, and Jean began to feel like a maid…." He sighed. "I've never seen anything like it. But I guess you have."

"Some of it anyway. It's never a happy situation."

"So anyway, my reputation began to suffer, my business began to suffer and by the time I figured out just how bad it was all really getting, Jean threatened to leave. So I made my choice."

Holly wanted to reach out and touch his arm in a gesture of sympathy, but resisted. Lisa might be watching, and there was no telling what that might precipitate.

"Well," she said after a moment, "I did offer her a room. I don't want anyone to sleep in a car if I can avoid it. Since I'm not in love with her, dealing with her ought to be easier for me. I've met the type, if not the exact version."

"You're kindhearted," he said. "You took her in so she wouldn't have to sleep in a car?"

"Anyone would."

"A stranger? But apart from that, don't be so kindhearted that she takes advantage of you. And don't let her know Martha left you any money, or she'll find a way to wheedle something out of you."

Holly laughed. She couldn't help it. "News flash, Cliff. I've dealt with manipulative people before. The hardest part of being a social worker in the early days, aside from the horrors you see, is realizing that some of those cute, sweet kids you want to help are master manipulators. It's survival and they learn it early." She paused. "I take it Lisa didn't grow up here?"

"No. She came to town with her parents. Her dad was a lawyer and he was working for some big development company."

"The ones who have the sign outside town about the ski resort?"

"Yeah, the ski resort that's never going to happen. Anyway, he was here about three months trying to work things out with the county and forest service. Long enough for me to get in serious trouble."

"I wonder why she came to you instead of Daddy."

"I haven't a clue. Maybe he had enough of her, too."

"Did she give you any idea of why she came here now?"

"Apparently she's not only between jobs but between marriages." He sighed. "I swear I'll try to find another arrangement for her. I'd already told her she could stay for a few days with me. I figured that would give me time to sort something out."

Holly felt a grin split her face. "Did you have to beg Jean?"

"Practically. Which reminds me, she sent over dinner for the two of you. She figured Lisa wouldn't do anything about it and she thought it was a damn shame you should have to."

"That's really nice! I always thought Jean was a sweetheart."

"She is. She was also a good friend of Martha's."

They started walking back toward the house and Holly couldn't resist saying, "I guess Martha left out all the good gossip."

"Martha never gossiped," he said drily. "It's probably why she had so many friends all her life. Listen, call me if Lisa gets to be too much."

"What can you do?"

"Throw her over my shoulder and carry her out of here? Hell, I don't know. Just don't let her get around your kindness again. She's a taker, Holly. Not a giver like you."

Which, when she thought about it, was probably the

nicest thing he'd said to her since she had returned. Maybe they'd get over the hump after all.

But as she watched him walk to his truck to pull out a cooler, she knew there was one hump she wasn't going to get over. She still wanted that man. She wanted him as much as she had from the first all those years ago. The sight of his narrow hips cased in denim as he walked away from her was enough to bring back memories of touching and holding him. Feeling him fill her, feeling...

"He's not worth mooning over," Lisa said. "He's not a very nice person."

Holly had to resist an urge to snap at her. "It hardly matters," she said quietly. "I'm going home in ten days. Like I told you."

The words were true, but a different truth seemed to impact her heart. She wasn't quite as eager to get away from Cliff as she had been even this morning.

That realization disturbed her more than Lisa's presence.

Then Cliff astonished her out of her thoughts. "I'm staying for dinner," he announced as he walked toward them with the cooler. "Jean sent plenty."

"Why?" Lisa demanded. "You think your friend here needs protection? Funny, I never saw you as a watchdog."

"No, just a lapdog," Cliff said as he passed her. Then, where Lisa couldn't see, he winked at Holly. "And by the way, my friend has a name. It's Holly."

Oh, man, Holly thought as she followed him into the house. This was going to be an interesting evening.

Lisa finally carried her own bags up the stairs. Holly was surprised at how small they were, not the kind of thing any healthy young woman should need help with. Clearly Lisa didn't need the help, because she didn't have the least struggle getting them upstairs all by herself.

Shrugging inwardly, she followed Cliff to the kitchen. He unloaded the contents of the ice chest. "There's enough in here for a few days. I'll take you to the grocery tomorrow if you like."

"I can find my way."

He paused and looked at her. "Do you ever let anyone help you?"

"You helped me with the tree."

"Because I didn't let you escape it. I want to help. I could help with a whole lot around here. Including my ex."

Holly couldn't help an almost furtive giggle. "She's really got you on edge."

"I'm more on edge because she's here with you. Bad enough having Jean put up with her, but Jean has experience. You have no idea about Lisa."

"So what should I expect?"

"Lisa doesn't cook, doesn't clean, doesn't pick up after herself, doesn't do laundry… In fact, all she likes to do is ride horses. Crap, I guess that means I'll deal with her every day anyway."

"She'll come to borrow a horse?"

"Probably. It'd be nice if she would take care of them, too."

A short silence fell as they put food away. Fried chicken. Potato salad. A whole host of filling foods, almost enough for an army. From above they heard some banging around.

"I guess she *does* unpack," Holly remarked.

Cliff paused then broke into a hearty laugh. "Evidently. Although not cheerfully."

He surprised her by reaching for her hand and holding it. Holly almost jerked from the electric zap that ran straight to her core. Oh, damn, she didn't want this. Or maybe she wanted it, but she didn't need it.

Cliff spoke. "I wish she hadn't come here. Maybe she can behave reasonably well for a few days. She used to know how, but that all depends on what she thinks she can get out of it. Now that she's got a room, she might not care what you think of her. I don't know."

"I've dealt with worse," she assured him.

His turquoise eyes held hers. "I guess you have. Did you give any more thought to having some of your kids out here?"

He dropped her hand, leaving her feeling bereft. Even that simple touch reminded her of how much she had given up when she left him to pursue her dream.

"Actually, I have." She had to clear her throat, as it felt oddly tight. "I'd just begun to consider it after what you said. Of course, there are a million hurdles, but I could see it in my mind's eye." She heard the growing excitement in her own voice. "It could be so great."

He put the lid back on the ice chest and set it near the door. "I hear a *but* in there."

"I think I need to talk to a friend of mine, Laurie. She's a child psychologist."

"Why? What worries you?"

She met his gaze, feeling her smile fade. "Taking those kids and showing them life out here, then throwing them back onto the same city streets? I'm not sure it would be good in every case."

"Don't some of these kids already go to camps of different kinds?"

"Some do. I just need to get advice on the right way to do it so that it's helpful, not harmful."

"Makes sense. It's something that never would have occurred to me. I guess that's why you're the social worker. I was just thinking how great it would be for kids in the city to spend some time on a minifarm."

"Oh, it would!" She felt her excitement return. "I could see having a vegetable garden, maybe a few sheep or goats, bunkhouses for them. But I'd have to come up with a whole raft of confidence-building ideas for them, maybe get some trained counselors to participate…but that's the end idea, the big idea. First I think I'd have to start pretty small."

She was bubbling again with the ideas that had been percolating before Lisa had showed up. "Maybe I'll have them stay for the entire summer break."

"That might be good. And don't give up on winter. We have Nordic skiing, sledding and ice-skating. Hell, I could make you a skating rink out back over the garden plot. And there's a new guy up north of here. He bought out the old Olmstead place and is running sled-dog trips over the winter. I bet you could get him interested, and he might even like some helping hands from time to time."

Her eagerness was growing by leaps. It always helped to find that someone else thought an idea was good. "Really? You'd help?"

"Of course I would."

Lisa's voice startled them both. "Of course he'll help," she said with acid in her voice. "He's quick to promise and quick to change his mind."

Whatever she might have thought of Cliff in the past, in that instant Holly's heart went out to him. She saw his face tighten, saw his brilliant eyes darken. He appeared all too much like a man taking another lash from a familiar whip.

Before he could respond, Holly turned to Lisa. "I don't remember including you in this discussion. How about we have some ground rules if you want to stay here? First, you look after yourself. Second, if you don't have something nice to say, don't say it."

"Or what?" Lisa demanded.

"Or I'll throw you out."

Lisa rolled her eyes. "Yeah, right."

"Listen," Holly said calmly, "I've dealt with a lot worse than you. This is *my* house, so it's *my* rules. Live by them or leave. And yes, I can throw you out. Easily."

Lisa glared, then flounced out the front door, slamming it behind her.

"Bravo," Cliff said quietly.

"She's actually quite breathtaking," Holly admitted. "She doesn't know me, but she's carrying on like this. And no, I'm not going to ask."

"Ask away. The answer is no, she wasn't this petulant when we were dating. So she *does* know how to behave."

"Only when she wants something, evidently. I guess she really does believe I won't throw her out, so she has all she wants from me."

"Damn, Holly. I don't want you to have to put up with this. I swear I'm going to find another solution."

"It's just ten days. I've dealt with worse, believe me. We'll either jolt along or she can clear out."

His frown darkened his whole face; he looked as if he wanted to say something, but chose not to. Finally he asked, "So is it all right if I stay for dinner? I can take some of the load off you."

"It's up to you." The truth was, she wanted him to

stay. Funny how she'd changed her perspective so fast, at least when it came to Cliff. But even as she was trying to act casual about it, she wondered why. Was that any way to respond to a courteous offer? Or was she just so damned determined to be independent that she could be unintentionally rude? It was possible. Life had toughened her quite a bit out of necessity. She wrapped her heart up to keep the pain at a distance, to avoid being used.

"I'd like you to stay," she said quickly. "Really. But from what I've seen, that's a lot to ask."

He surprised her with a short laugh. "I've dealt with her before. I was prepared to deal with her for a few days. I can't imagine why she came hotfooting over here. She didn't need to."

Holly tilted her head. "You're right."

"So that leaves me wondering what she's really up to."

"Maybe it was spur of the moment when she saw me."

Cliff shrugged. "I guess anything's possible. I'll never understand her, that's for sure. I can often predict her, but I don't understand her."

That, thought Holly, was probably the most succinct description she'd ever heard of a problematic relationship, and a good measure of what Cliff had been through.

She actually felt sorry for him.

Chapter Five

Holly asked if they should wait for Lisa. Cliff rebelled immediately. He supposed he wasn't presenting himself in the best light, but too bad. Holly didn't care about him anyway. As for Lisa, his answer was simple: "Best to start the way you mean to continue. You've got plenty to do over the time you have left. I'll be glad to help as much as I can. But don't start treating Lisa like a guest or you'll regret it. If I'd had any idea, I wouldn't have been such a pushover in the early days."

He caught the twinkle in her eye. Was she warming to him? When he was acting like an ungentlemanly jerk? He had the worst urge to just sweep her into a hug and kiss her until she was breathless. The way he once had. But look where that had gotten him.

"You? A pushover?" She gave him a gentle shove on the shoulder with her palm. "Okay, then. Let's just fill our own plates. It was so nice of Jean to think of this."

"I think Jean was feeling a great deal of sympathy for you."

"So she really did mutiny?"

"Believe it." He found the plates in the cupboard, still where Martha kept them, and pulled them out while Holly got silverware. "I've never seen her as furious as she was the day she decided she had had enough. She followed me into my office at the end of the day and let fly. Honestly, she'd been keeping so much to herself that I had no idea how bad it had gotten."

"But you'd already had some of your men leave, right?"

"Oh, yeah. They weren't paid to carry shopping bags, or plant flowers she bought, or... Well, it was a pretty long list, all of it full of things I hadn't hired them to do. So they left, one after another, as soon as they found other work. Meanwhile, I was going nuts with the bank, the money and all the rest. They didn't want to be personal servants and I didn't want to lose the ranch. Then Jean."

"What did she say?"

"That she couldn't stand watching me be treated this way. That was her major thing, I guess."

"I can understand that." They sat at the table with plates of fried chicken, potato salad and glasses of iced tea.

"But there was other stuff, too, little stuff that must have been chapping her for a while. Having to pick up wet towels and dirty clothes in the bathroom and bedroom. Dirty dishes and cups left all over the house. Cleaning up spills. Ironing whatever Lisa wanted to wear at that moment. The list went on. I don't even remember it all. The main thing that struck me was her insistence that she couldn't stand to watch Lisa take advantage of me, and that she'd have to leave if things didn't change."

Holly paused as she put her fork into the potato salad on her plate. "I'm sorry. It must have hurt to hear all that."

"I was past being hurt. I was mad most of the time. I knew something had to give, but I'd said those vows, you know."

Holly nodded. He thought she looked pained. For him? The idea shocked him. "I've watched plenty of people break up over less," she said slowly. "But I'll say again, her behavior was abusive."

"Maybe so. But now it's in your house. Damn it."

As they ate, he wondered how the hell this had happened. He had told Lisa she could stay for a few days until he figured something else. What had caused her to move in on Holly?

He had a thought that caused him to pause in midbite. "You," he said.

"Me what?"

"She said she came over here looking for Martha. But what if she'd heard something about the two of us?"

"I thought we were pretty secretive." She colored faintly. "I'd have sworn nobody knew but Martha, and maybe Jean."

"Martha never missed a thing. But what if somebody else had mentioned how close we were that summer?"

"It's possible. I mean, we did go out a few times with your friends."

"So she could have guessed."

Holly nodded. "Still…"

"What if she said something to Jean about staying with Martha? It'd be just like Jean to tell her to forget that, because Martha had passed and you owned the house now."

He watched Holly's eyes widen. "It would fit her pattern of trying to keep you away from your friends."

"Her pattern of trying to spread nastiness about me."

"Either way." Holly resumed eating. He realized that he was sitting there staring at her as if he was moonstruck. He'd better stop it. That time had come and gone.

He finished a few more mouthfuls of chicken, then asked, "What makes people act that way?"

"I can't be certain about Lisa because I just met her. But generally speaking, I think a lot of them must be control freaks. Extreme control freaks. She wanted you cut off so you had no support system. She wanted everyone else to do her bidding and if they left, so much the better for her, because then she'd have total control."

"I wasn't going to cook or clean for her."

"No, but if Jean left, she could hire someone and then she'd have control. She couldn't completely control Jean because she knew you'd never get rid of her. So she sought other ways of getting rid of her."

"Crap."

"I'm just guessing," Holly said. "I've had some psychology training, obviously, and this is also based on my observations of abusive relationships."

"I guess you've seen more than a few."

"I have. Trying to convince someone to get out of a relationship like that can be difficult, because the victim is steadily trained to feel responsible for everything that displeases the abuser. I guess you were strong enough to withstand it for two years."

"I'd have been stronger if I'd gotten rid of her sooner."

She astonished him by putting her fork down and reaching across the table to clasp his hand. "Love is a dangerous thing," she said quietly. "All of us begin with a huge desire to please the one we love. If one of the parties is unscrupulous, the other one can wind up in trouble. I don't think you were weak. Far from it. You got mad and got out. Congratulations."

He turned his hand over to clasp hers and their eyes met. She had such beautiful blue eyes, he thought. The years had thinned her too much, but she was still every bit as gorgeous as she had been a decade ago when he had believed the only thing he wanted in life was a future with Holly.

Looking into her eyes, he had that impulse again. His entire body began to sizzle, and he felt his groin grow heavy with desire. Her eyes darkened and he recognized her response to him. She still wanted him, too.

Before he could remind himself there was no future in it, a sarcastic voice said from the kitchen doorway, "My, isn't this cozy."

Holly snapped her hand back as if she'd been scalded. Cliff felt the surge of an old, familiar anger. Right then he'd have loved nothing more than to carry that woman out to her car, throw her clothes in after her and tell her to get lost for good.

"I don't get invited to dinner?" Lisa asked. "What a rude way to treat a guest."

Cliff stood and faced her. "You're not a guest here. You're a stray that a kind lady offered to take in for a few days. She could change her mind and I wouldn't blame her. So find your own food in the fridge and feed yourself. You can do at least that much on your own, can't you?"

He turned back to Holly and was surprised to see a faint smile dancing around the corners of her mouth.

"Would you like to take a walk and finish eating later when the company is more pleasant?"

Holly rose instantly. "I'd love to." Her smile became visible.

Cliff held out his hand and to his amazement, she took it. They grabbed jackets from the mudroom, because spring evenings cooled down quite a bit, and stepped out back.

"I'm sorry," he said when they'd left the house a few yards behind. "I probably just made it worse for you."

She shook her head. "It's okay. I've dealt with tougher nuts. Gang members. Street fighters. Men who were pummeling their wives or kids. She doesn't scare me."

He took her hand again, squeezing her fingers. "I can't imagine what you've seen or been through."

"Good. Not everyone needs to. So, if Lisa hadn't turned up, it would have been nice to use you as a sounding board about this camp idea."

"We can do that anyway. Maybe if we ignore her enough, she'll leave. You know what occurred to me today as I was working? Before Lisa arrived, anyway."

"What's that?"

He drew a deep breath, preparing for any kind of response, and said, "I'd have loved to take you riding, visit some of our old haunts."

He half expected her to get angry for bringing up that long-ago summer. Especially when he'd initially been so cold to her when she returned.

He heard her sigh. "Cliff, you can't go back in time."

"I know that. But we had a wonderful summer and sometimes I go to our places and just remember it. Good memories are rare enough in this life."

She stopped walking and faced him. "Really? You do that?"

"There's only one part of it that wasn't good. Why the hell would I want to forget?"

She looked down at her feet. "I try hard not to, but sometimes I think about it, too," she admitted quietly. "On nights when I start to feel worn-out or burned-out. I'm not complaining, mind you. I chose the life I needed, and I'm sorry my choice hurt you, but yeah, sometimes I remember. I was happier then than I've ever been."

He supposed he could be content knowing that. His memories weren't addled. "Me, too," he said quietly. "Me, too."

Another look passed between them, this one almost smoldering. It was a fire they couldn't douse with Lisa in the house nearby, and now he had a new reason to curse his ex. On the other hand, it was probably best that they couldn't. She intended to go back to her job. Neither of them needed a repeat of the summer long ago, and sex wasn't enough. It was never enough.

He was just getting to know this Holly. Best not to muddle things any more than they already were.

He dragged his gaze away, and they walked farther along the fence line. "These leases…" he said.

"Yours, you mean?"

"Yeah. If you need more room, you could use some of the land. I don't need every square inch of it. But I do need most of it. It's allowed me to expand my operation because of the added grazing. The ranch is actually turning a profit, not an easy thing to do these days. But you're talking about bunkhouses and things like that. You might need more room."

"That's a long way down the road," she answered. "But that's a generous offer. Thank you."

"It might not be as far down the road as you think.

We could transform this place pretty fast. The main thing you need to do is figure out what you need."

"And figure out the red tape."

He was glad to see her brightening again. He wanted to know more about her life in Chicago, about the things that had brought her here looking so worn, but he didn't feel he had the right to get so personal. Not yet, maybe never.

Ten days, he reminded himself. She was leaving in ten days. She kept mentioning it, maybe as a warning. Evidently she didn't want to repeat the mistakes of their long-ago summer romance.

Except, much as it had hurt him in the end, he just couldn't think of it as a mistake. But maybe it had been for her. She hadn't accepted his offer to visit some of their old haunts, even though she'd admitted to treasuring at least some of the memories.

Maybe for her it hadn't meant what it had meant for him at the time. Maybe her heart hadn't been in it. Maybe for her it had been just a fling.

The thought soured his mouth and stomach. *Be smart,* he told himself. *Keep your guard up.* It was possible to be helpful without going any further.

Maybe for once in his life it was time not to throw his entire being into something. For sure, the only thing he gave his all to that had never betrayed him was his ranch.

It would be wise to remember that.

Cliff headed out an hour later with a handwritten thank-you note from Holly for Jean. She stood in the doorway watching him drive away, feeling as if something really important had happened, as if the ground beneath her feet had shifted in some way.

She had certainly seen a side of Cliff she'd never imagined. He had survived a poisonous relationship; he seemed firmer and steadier than she remembered him being. He had certainly grown up well. And he had evidently turned into a protector. Imagine him spending all this time here just to try to keep Lisa in line. That had to have been uncomfortable for him, even after all these years.

Her attraction to him hadn't faded one little bit, either. Maybe he was even more attractive now. It was pointless to give in to it, but considering she hadn't felt any attraction to a man since she was attacked last year, it was good to know she still could respond this way.

"How do I get wash done?"

Holly turned slowly, closing the door on the night and preparing to deal with Lisa. "Laundry?"

"That's what I said."

"Well," Holly said slowly, "there are machines at the back of the house. Help yourself. If you want someone to do it for you, I think there's a laundry in town where they charge by the load for washing, drying and folding. I'm not sure they also do ironing."

Lisa frowned.

Holly smiled politely, then headed for the living room. She needed to find something to read, a wall to put up between her and this woman. She had a feeling she was going to regret taking Lisa in more than she had ever regretted providing shelter to someone in trouble numerous times in the past.

Lisa wasn't really in trouble. She *was* trouble.

Unfortunately, the woman followed her into the living room. "I can't afford to pay someone to do my wash."

"Like I said, there are machines in the back of the

house." Holly sat in her aunt's rocker and reached for a magazine. Something about embroidery. She'd never had time for that.

"I'll need help," Lisa said.

Holly looked up. "Really? You don't know how to do laundry? I've worked with *children* who do laundry for their entire families."

"You're mean."

"If I were mean, you wouldn't be staying here." Holly returned her attention to the magazine.

But Lisa wasn't ready to go away. "I saw how you looked at Cliff. You have the hots for him." She sat on the sofa facing Holly.

"Really?" Holly tried to sound disinterested.

"Well, he's a looker. I fell for it, too."

Holly arched her brow, but refused to take her attention from the magazine. Her heart had sped up, and she could feel her annoyance building. Was this woman trying to precipitate a fight? "Looks aren't everything."

"They certainly aren't. That man should have married his ranch instead of me. He's nailed to the place."

"Seems to be the usual thing for ranchers."

"When we first got married, he'd take me to Denver for the weekend sometimes, but then that stopped. He said it was too expensive. So I went by myself. Then he got mad because I bought clothes and got my hair and nails done. It wasn't like I was buying fancy jewelry or something."

"Hmm."

Silence for a blessed minute or two. Just as Holly dared to hope it would continue, Lisa spoke again. "So did you ever live here?"

"No. Just visited my aunt."

"She was a strange bird."

At that, Holly's head snapped up. She put the magazine aside. "Are you looking for a way to make me angry? Because you're close to succeeding, and if I can't have you around here without me getting angry, you're going to be leaving. I'm torn up enough about my aunt's passing. I don't need you to pile on. Find another way to entertain yourself."

"Out here in the middle of nowhere?"

"You have a car." With that Holly rose and headed upstairs. Enough was enough.

How the heck had Cliff survived this for two years? She couldn't stand it for one evening.

Upstairs, she pulled out a book, climbed into her pajamas, then forgot all about reading as she stared out the window into the night. Cliff wouldn't be riding this direction tonight, she thought.

She remembered what he had said about occasionally visiting their old haunts. Her cheeks heated a bit because she knew exactly what haunts he meant. Like young, healthy animals, they'd made love anywhere and everywhere they could find the privacy. Looking back at it, she was surprised at how voracious they'd both been. Oh, they'd had fun, and laughed a lot, but they'd also been insatiable.

She leaned her forehead against the cool glass, remembering, and wondering if that hadn't had something to do with her reluctance to stay with Cliff so long ago. Even at the age of twenty it had seemed to her that you needed more than sex for an enduring relationship.

But in all honesty, it wasn't just that. She had things she wanted to do, things she couldn't do as a ranch wife. Back then it had looked like a kind of dead end.

Right now, it looked like heaven on earth. She almost laughed aloud at herself. She was just tired. She'd been fighting burnout before she got here, before her aunt died. She had definitely needed a break, and right now this place was providing peace and relaxation. Well, except for Lisa, and that woman didn't come close to the stressors she faced on her job.

Hell, she felt guilty from being away from her kids for even two weeks. She tried to maintain a professional distance, had even gotten better at it, but she still cared. Deep in her being, she cared about those kids and their families.

But she also remembered something one of her colleagues had said a month or so ago: "Holly, you need a break. Take some desk time, rotate into another area. If you don't, you're going to be useless to everyone."

She had acknowledged the justice of what Carla had said, but hadn't taken any action to rotate into something less taxing. Stubbornness? Hubris? She didn't know. Certainly most of her other colleagues were capable of stepping in for her, capable of looking after her clients.

So what was it with her? Maybe she hadn't realized how close to the edge she was getting? Certainly, not until she got here and felt the weight lifting from her had she realized that she was tense in every fiber of her being.

Cliff's words floated back to her, about her reluctance to let anyone help her. Maybe that was at the rock bottom of it all. She put her mind to something and let nothing deter her. That had cost her Cliff, and now it might be harming her health.

She turned and caught sight of herself in the mirror over the dresser. She'd lost twenty pounds since the attack. Some of them she had needed to lose, but the woman who stared back at her right now looked almost hollow.

Quickly she turned back to the window, concealing her reflection there by pressing her forehead to the glass again.

Maybe she had a lot more to deal with than just her grief over Martha and closing this place up. Maybe she needed to deal with things deep inside her that drove her mercilessly.

There was really no reason for it. She'd had a normal, happy childhood. Well, as normal as the child of parents in the diplomatic corps could have. She'd bounced around the world, but had always thrived on the changes. It was during those travels that she had developed a deep ache in her soul for the world's suffering innocents. It was that experience that had driven her into social work.

But still, Carla was right. If she didn't take a break, she'd wind up being useless to the very people she most wanted to help.

Maybe her dedication was more than dedication. Maybe some of those starving children she had seen around the world had become a demon that drove her, yielding to no reason.

One thing for sure, she had never forgotten their faces. Their hunger. The rags they wore. Her parents had tried to shield her from the worst of it, but they hadn't always succeeded. While she'd never been in a war zone—her parents wouldn't have been allowed to take their daughter into one, even had they wanted to—she'd been in many countries that could easily be called famine, disease and neglect.

The same famine, disease and neglect that collected in pockets in this country like untreated sores. And always, always she felt the anger than she couldn't do more.

Her mental mirror was proving no more comfortable than the one above the dresser. How many times in training had she been warned that she needed to keep a distance, reserve time for herself and turn it all off when she went home at night? That she could lose her effectiveness if she didn't? That she could make herself seriously ill if she didn't care for herself.

Damn, she thought, closing her eyes. Maybe *she* needed a caretaker. Clearly she wasn't doing the job for herself.

Then another thought struck her. Her head snapped up and she scrambled for the extension phone beside the bed. Thank God it had a list of numbers on autodial, even though her aunt had seldom used this room. Martha must have been getting worried that something could happen to her at any time.

"God, Martha," she said out loud. "Why didn't you call me?"

Because she would have come running at the drop of a hat if Martha had needed her.

She hit the button labeled *Cliff* and listened to it ring. At last he answered.

"Martin Ranch."

"Cliff? Cliff, it's Holly. I need you, please. Meet me out back by the fence."

"Want me to bring a horse for you or drive?"

"I don't care. I just need you."

"On my way."

There was a click and the line went dead.

It was too damn cold, and high clouds had moved in overhead, turning the night dark as pitch. It was not a night for riding hell-for-leather over open ground, so Cliff hopped into his truck.

Holly had sounded tense, but not in pain, so he assumed Lisa must have finally found a button to push. If so, that woman was going to be out of there on her butt before the sun rose if he had to call the sheriff to do it.

Damn, he should never have left the two of them alone. But what the hell was he supposed to do? He had no right to override Holly's decision to ask Lisa to stay. Not his house.

The drive seemed to take forever, although at the speed he was going he should have gotten a half dozen tickets. Still, it took him twenty minutes to arrive, and he hit the brakes so hard at the end of the gravel drive that he skidded.

Out by the back fence. So he set out at a dead run until he saw the ghostly figure of Holly standing out there alone.

"Holly?" he asked quietly, slowing his approach.

"I'm sorry," she said tautly. "I'm sorry. You didn't need to race. I should have told you, but…" Her voice broke.

That sound did him in. He didn't care about the past, about the future, about whether Lisa saw and found additional reasons to be nasty. He just stepped into her and wrapped her in a bear hug as tightly as he dared, his chin coming to rest on her sweet-smelling hair. "What?" he asked, trying to shift from the fury that had been building in him to the gentleness he needed now.

"I need…I need to talk," she said brokenly, then burst into wrenching sobs.

He didn't ask any questions. She couldn't have answered anyway, and for right now he felt deep inside that she just needed to be held and comforted, whatever was going on. He could do that much.

God, it felt so good to hold her again. He rubbed her back, feeling his own chest tighten in response to her pain. Gradually she began to quiet and he dared to speak.

"Want to go for a drive or over to my place?"

She drew a sharp, choked breath. "Yeah," she whispered. "Away."

So he took her away.

He drove more slowly this time and decided to take her to his place. It'd be more comfortable and they'd have the privacy she seemed to want. Why else had she stood at the back fence alone?

He wanted to ask if Lisa had done something but kept quiet. Let her talk in her own time, when she was ready. She didn't need any pressure from him.

She remained hunched beside him, her arms wrapped tightly around herself as if she were holding something in. He doubted Lisa could have done anything to make her feel that bad. God, she had said she wanted to talk; he couldn't help in any way unless she talked and here they were, barreling through the night in silence.

He forced a lid on his impatience, reminding himself that she had called out to him and now the best thing he could do was give her space and time until she let him know what else she needed.

At least she'd called him. Turned to him as a friend. A week ago he would have said he never wanted to see her again. Now here he was all wrapped up in her with no idea whether he'd be left like roadkill again.

Okay, maybe that wasn't entirely fair, but it was how he had felt. He could look back now and see how egotistical he'd been. He'd ignored all her intentions to pursue a career, just so absolutely certain she wouldn't be able to say no to his proposal. Certain she loved him enough to spend the rest of her life here, with him. She hadn't misled him—he'd misled himself.

Not until the lights of his house appeared out of the darkness did she speak. "Your ranch?"

"I figured it was warmer and more comfortable than this truck. Plus, I can get you something hot to drink."

"Thanks."

Her voice sounded steadier to him now, and that was a huge relief. He brought them to a stop at the front door. Hardly had he turned off the ignition when Jean stepped out.

"Everything okay?" she called.

"Fine," Cliff answered. "I brought Holly over for a visit."

He walked around the truck to help Holly out. She didn't resist, and moments later Jean had enveloped her, leaving Cliff to stand there bemused, keys in hand. Well, maybe it was woman stuff. Maybe Holly would rather talk to Jean. Crazy, but he felt as if he'd just been cut off at the pass.

Chapter Six

Holly was beginning to feel stupid. She'd called Cliff out late at night because she was having an emotional crisis? She should have called Laurie or Carla or Sharon. And now elderly, gray-haired Jean was fussing over her like a mother hen, getting her settled in the living room, asking what she wanted to drink.

It was embarrassing. She had reached out because she needed not to be alone, and now she was surrounded by caretakers, with a man who was certainly going to want some kind of explanation, whether or not she felt like talking about it now.

She accepted the offer of tea with honey, thinking that she should have just handled her emotional storm by herself. The way she usually did. She could have walked it off. What had possessed her to call a man who had absolutely no reason to want to be her confidant?

But he had come racing to the rescue nonetheless,

and that hug he had given her had meant the world. All by itself it had been healing. She wondered how she could possibly thank him.

"I'm going to bed," Jean announced. She bent to give Holly another quick hug. "Cliff knows where everything is if you need something. The guest room is ready, too, if you want to stay."

Not a word about Lisa. A coded message, perhaps? Maybe Jean thought she was here because of something Lisa had done. Boy, would she like to leave it that way.

She gave Cliff credit, though, for not pushing her in any way. Hell, he hadn't even asked a single question, which was kind of amazing considering the way she had called him and then sobbed in his arms. He must want to know what all this was about, but now that she was looking at him, she wasn't sure she could explain it.

She curled in one corner of a big leather couch. He'd settled in a matching chair facing her and sat forward with his elbows on his splayed knees and hands clasped. He ignored the tea Jean had put on the table at his elbow.

"Feeling a little better?" he asked finally.

"I'm sorry I called you." The words burst from her.

He lifted his brows, but didn't move. Those darn turquoise eyes of his kept right on looking at her. She wished she had a hole to crawl into.

"I hope," he said, "that you mean you're sorry for bothering me, not that you're sorry I came."

Ouch! She grabbed a throw pillow and hugged it, staring down at it because it was easier. "I'm sorry I bothered you."

"No need. It was no bother at all. Obviously you needed someone. Excuse me, but I just can't imagine you dumping those tears on Lisa."

In spite of herself, she saw the humor in the notion.

"Uh, no," she said finally. "But I'm still sorry to have bothered you. Honestly, I should be able to deal with things myself, not call you out late at night."

"It's not that late. And the amazing thing is, well…" He paused. "My mother always used to say that a joy shared was a joy multiplied. I think it goes the other way, too—a burden shared is a burden lightened. That's what friends are for, right?"

"Are we friends?" That burst from her, too, and she began to wonder seriously about the state of her mind. What was she doing? What was she trying to get at with him?

"I think we're getting back to friendship," he said. "Admittedly, we avoided each other like the plague for the past ten years. Admittedly, when I saw you at the lawyer's office I was nasty. I think there was a buildup of things not said a long time ago."

"Then maybe you should say them."

"Why? That *was* a long time ago. Anyway, this isn't about me, it isn't about us. Is it?"

She shook her head, pulling on the fringe that rimmed the pillow.

"Was it Lisa?"

"That woman couldn't push me to that point. Ever."

"Then…?"

Holly sighed, darting a glance his way. Damn, he looked concerned and sympathetic. "I was just thinking generally about things. About myself."

"And?"

She picked at the pillow some more, then tossed it aside. "I was thinking about how driven I am. Some of my colleagues have been pushing me to take a rotation to an easier job for a while. It's not unusual. Casework, the kind that takes you on the streets and into homes, can get to you. They even warned us to leave the job at work and not bring it home."

"Why do I think you find that difficult?"

She gave him a humorless half smile. "I guess you know me."

"A little, anyway. So even your colleagues think you need a rotation?"

"Yeah. And I haven't been listening. And that got me to thinking about why social work was so important to me, and just what demons might be driving me."

"I gather the answer upset you."

"Very much." She was grateful that he didn't press her, just waited for whatever she wanted to say. At this point she didn't know. "It's quite a mess," she said finally. "Hard to explain. But then I made a link I hadn't made before and I kinda fell apart." That part embarrassed her. She was tougher than that, right? Well, maybe not, and it appalled her to be faced with her own weakness.

"There are," she said slowly, "a lot of good social workers. I could name a dozen right off the top of my head who could take care of my clients. They'd do a fine job. There's no *need* for me to feel like I can't turn it over to someone else for a little while."

"Are you worrying about your relationship with the children?"

"A little. You develop them, you know. No matter how hard you try to maintain a professional distance, a balance, with at least some of those kids you become a trusted person, someone they can rely on. To just shift myself out of the picture, even if only for a month or so, might not be good."

He hesitated. "You came out here for two weeks. You explained to them, right?"

She nodded.

"Are any of them too young to understand that you need to go away for a little while but that you'll be back?"

"Probably not. And that's when I looked hard at myself. Just by its very nature, social work results in kids and their families getting different caseworkers from time to time. We try to ease the transition, both of us showing up together at least once, but it happens all the time."

"So the kids get it. You're not a parent but a professional they work with."

"Yeah, and that's what makes what I'm doing so ridiculous. It's not like I'm the fairy godmother with the only magic wand in town. I started thinking that I'm getting too full of myself. Started feeling too important. The truth is, if I dropped off the earth tomorrow, plenty of competent people would step in to help my clients and they'd be just fine."

"Maybe so. Aren't you being a little hard on yourself? I mean, you care. That's not something to apologize for."

"Another thing they warn us about is that if we don't take care of ourselves, we won't be able to take care of anybody else. I've been pushing that line for the past year. Driven. Driven to the point that my colleagues are commenting. That's bad."

"Wouldn't a supervisor step in?"

"If we weren't always so shorthanded, maybe. Right now, if I rotate, I'll probably increase someone else's load."

He gave a low whistle. "That's a rock and a hard place all around."

"But it's not the whole story. I've been taking my

work home with me. I think about nothing else anymore. So anyway, as I was standing in the bedroom, I caught sight of myself in the mirror. I've lost twenty pounds in the past year."

"I noticed. A little too much?"

"Too much. Five pounds needed to go. Maybe even ten. But not twenty."

He waited, and she got the feeling he wasn't going to accept her weight loss as an excuse for her tears. She sighed again and put her head down. When her voice emerged, it was muffled. "That's when I made the connection."

"To what?"

"To the attack a year ago. I've been avoiding dealing with it by working myself to death. By letting my job consume me. It was easier. Yes, easier. I got sick of people saying how strong I was because I came back to work two weeks later. Because it wasn't true. I was a scared, nervous wreck, and I think tonight I finally had the breakdown I should have had back then."

There, it was out. She'd admitted that she was a coward, that she couldn't deal with what had happened to her and that she was driven not as much by concern for her clients as by a need to escape her own mind and emotions.

From where she sat, that was a pretty ugly, cowardly thing.

Worse, she felt she had just revealed something sordid to Cliff. This wasn't a light she wanted him to see her in. Then another thought struck her. Why should she feel sordid about what had been done to her? God, she was losing it.

"Holly?"

His voice pulled her back from a dark cliff. She dared to look at him.

"I'm not asking for details here. I'm not an inquisitor or a prosecutor. Hell, I'm just an ordinary guy who probably knows more about sheep and goats than people. But can you give me an outline of what happened? Martha just said you were attacked but you were okay. I'd like to know generally what we're talking about here."

She closed her eyes.

"You don't have to tell me if it's too painful."

"I think," she said in a thin voice, "that facing this is exactly what my mind is trying to tell me to do. I can't bury it any longer."

He waited, giving her space and time to gather herself enough to look into that black pit she'd been avoiding for a year now.

"I stayed out way too late. Not that that area of town is exactly safe in broad daylight, but I stayed too long with a client. They were having some serious trouble in that house and I was worried about violence erupting. Nothing had happened that I could call the police for. I mean, nobody got hit, nobody threatened anybody, but it was building that way, and I was trying to mediate and calm it down, and wondering if I should get the children out, at least for the night. Anyhow, I lost track of time."

She opened her eyes in time to see him nod.

"So when I came out of the complex, the streets were fairly empty, although not completely. They seldom are. But at least in the daytime, there are plenty of people out and about. It helps. But I knew I was in trouble when I was halfway to my car and all of sudden there was nobody at all on the street. They just melted away, except for three guys. I knew I needed to get to a safe place or into my car fast. I didn't make it." She fell silent, fighting for control as her heart hammered and her fists clenched so tightly her nails bit into her palms.

Cliff rose swiftly and came to sit right beside her. His powerful arm wrapped around her shoulders. She turned into him as if he were a bastion of safety.

"I was lucky," she said. "Very lucky. As soon as they grabbed for me, I started screaming my head off. They just laughed. They thought they had me. Except…" Her voice broke. "Do you know how much courage it took for someone in the surrounding buildings to call the cops? I do. I didn't expect it. I thought I was done."

"Why so courageous for someone to call?"

"Retaliation. It's another world, Cliff. People there don't dare call the police about much. Between gang retaliation and the way the cops themselves can behave, it's all too often a lose-lose situation for them."

"God!"

"But somebody called. And for once the cops did it right."

"What do you mean?"

"They didn't come in with a dozen cars, sirens screaming. They didn't give away that they had been called. I barely remember, I was down on the ground by then, but I heard this engine purr, and then the spotlight came on, and some time later there were a half dozen patrol cars there. It's all confused. You'd think something like that would be etched so clearly in my brain I couldn't forget a bit of it."

"Maybe not remembering is better."

"Maybe. I don't know. I remember the terror, I remember fighting as best I could, I even remember the way one guy's breath smelled. He was so damn drunk.

Anyway, I got off easy, with a few bruises and scrapes and some torn clothing."

"I don't know that I'd exactly call that getting off easy."

"Cliff, I was lucky. Very lucky because someone took a huge risk for me and called for help. I'll never know who it was. I'll never know who to thank."

He twisted a little and drew her closer, so that he could stroke her hair and cuddle her better. Liking it, she almost wanted to burrow into him.

"Maybe," he said slowly, "you need to think a little less about how lucky you were and face up to the fact that you suffered a horrible attack."

"That occurred to me tonight when I started thinking about how work obsessed I've become. I'm not leaving room for anything else."

"Not even eating, evidently."

She didn't answer for a few minutes. She was still trying to put pieces together in her mind. "I think I was putting myself in a prison of work because I was afraid of what was outside of it. Trying not to face what had happened to me. What could happen again. A lot of people were surprised I could go right back to work, that I didn't even ask for another neighborhood."

"You weren't going to let them defeat you, were you?"

"I guess not. Which is where my stubbornness comes in. I thought of it like getting back on the horse that threw you. Maybe I was afraid that if I gave in even a little bit, then the fear would grow and start encompassing more things."

"I suppose it might."

"But the end result is I never dealt with it, and to

avoid thinking about it, I've been working myself to the ragged edge. As if I could beat those guys that way."

"You might just be too brave and stubborn for your own good."

She fell silent, not certain she wanted to say more, unsure of how much she wanted to share with this man who had returned to her life only a few short days ago. At first he'd seemed so determined to dislike her but now... What had happened? Had he forgiven her? Had she forgiven herself? She felt so messed up right now that she didn't know what was really going on inside herself.

He began to rub her back gently, soothingly. She tucked her head into his shoulder and risked winding her arms around his waist. His offered comfort started to fill her.

Then he asked the question, the one that gave her no quarter. "So what are you really afraid of here, Holly? Except for not being able to bury yourself in work, nothing changed by you coming out here."

"Yes, it did," she said, unable to silence the words, no matter how hard it was to speak them. "I don't want to go back."

Holy hell, Cliff thought. That was momentous. It left him speechless. He knew as well as anyone how much being a social worker meant to this woman. The scars of her determination still resided in his heart. Come to that, the scars of her determination probably resided in her heart and soul.

He couldn't think of a damn thing to say. All he could do was hold her close and let her go wherever she wanted or needed to go with this. He wasn't comfortable with feeling helpless, but he felt utterly help-less right now.

He vastly preferred to deal with matters, get them taken care of, pleasant or not, and move on. Not that he'd been great about the moving-on part with Holly. He remembered moping for a long time.

But now he certainly understood why she had needed someone to talk to. Just thinking that she shouldn't go back would have rocked her to her very core. The attack was bad enough, and the single detail of the guy's breath was enough to tell him what they'd been after. He had to admit he was surprised that she'd been able to return to her work in that same neighborhood. He couldn't imagine.

As he sat there holding her, he thought about the protected life he'd led. Not exactly sheltered. He'd dealt with other exigencies, like bad years, range fires, the deaths of animals, plenty of hard times. Holding things together with twine and a prayer, he sometimes thought.

But nothing like what she had been facing. He felt so damn inadequate right now. He didn't know how to comfort her; he didn't have any helpful words, nothing to offer. Nothing except that he could hold her, and that seemed a small enough thing to do.

Before long, however, it ceased to be a small thing. Memories of that long-ago summer began to burgeon in his brain even as his body responded to her close-ness. There was an inevitability to it, as if she were the key to a lock that hadn't been opened in a long time. A key to feelings and sensations he had put away, only to discover that they hadn't even become dusty with time.

He was older now, though. He had learned some self-control, and some other basic truths, such as that anticipation had pleasures of its own.

The ache began to build in him, the need and the yearning, but he checked them. Now was certainly not the time. The time might never come again, but it certainly wasn't going to happen when she was in the middle of a crisis. Once he had been young enough to think that making love was an anodyne to everything. He was no longer that young.

Older and wiser, he might wish and want, but he could still maintain enough sense to know it wasn't right.

Although maintaining that sense was getting harder by the minute. His groin grew heavy and throbbed. His heart beat a little faster. His hands itched to reacquaint themselves with her every charm—charms he remembered as if they had been permanently etched on his brain and skin.

To him she had always been irresistible. When she had walked into the lawyer's office, he had realized in an instant that that hadn't changed, despite all the pain she had caused him. That's why he'd been so annoyed.

He'd long since learned a measure of forgiveness for her. She had left because she had other things to do, things that didn't involve being buried on a ranch. She'd never made any secret of that, she'd never misled him. He'd misled himself, and finally he had become man enough to admit it.

He had thought he was in love with her. Maybe he had been. But he wasn't in love now. He didn't know her well enough, and probably never would. She might talk about not wanting to go back, but she would. It was her life.

And he was too smart now to put himself in that bind again.

But he sure wouldn't have minded making love with

her again. Once, twice, a hundred times—the passion remained after all else was gone.

Kind of amazing, actually.

Right then he didn't dare move a muscle for fear he would make the wrong move. It would be so easy to kiss her, to fondle her, to pull her clothes away and bury himself in her welcoming depths. To reenact the folly of so long ago. A summer love, a time when he'd been high as a kite on her, and randy every single waking moment. They had frolicked endlessly and joyously.

And unrealistically. It had been a few months stolen from reality. He knew that now. Sooner or later, one way or another, reality would have intruded on their cocoon of laughter and passion.

It was intruding right now. The licking tongues of flame that devoured him and urged him to take her right this second couldn't have been more inappropriate.

He sighed and shifted cautiously, resigning himself to unsated need. Some things mattered more. He'd managed to grow up at least that much.

She stirred against him and for a second he froze as a rush of renewed hunger flooded him. He wished he knew what it was about her. Not even Lisa had ever managed to make him feel the kind of desire this woman kindled in him. Which was not to say he hadn't enjoyed Lisa, but Holly was in a whole different league.

He nearly voiced a protest when she eased out of his arms and sat back. Then she blew him away.

"I shouldn't do that," she said.

"Do what?"

"Let you hold me. All it does is make me crazy with wanting you again."

"Damn," he murmured. He clenched his fists and fought an urge to pounce on her right then.

"I guess I shouldn't have said that." She tried to jump up but he caught her wrist and stopped her.

"It's okay," he said. "I'm kind of feeling the same way." *Kind of?* He had fireworks going off in his head because of her admission.

"But we can't go back," she said.

"I know."

"I mean, how do I know what I'm feeling right now isn't just a memory?"

Memory? What he was feeling right now was no memory. Not by any stretch.

"Regardless," she said, giving him the sense that she was trying to be reasonable, "last time we let passion rule us, we got hurt. We'd be fools to open that door again."

She was probably right, but he was perilously close to not caring. He shut his eyes briefly, battering the caveman in him back to a darker corner, then looked at her again. He hadn't missed the fact that she had said, "*we* got hurt."

"Holly? Were you hurt, too, when you left?" This whole thing was beginning to take on some strange dimensions, and he had to figure it out.

"Of course I was."

"I wish I'd known that." He might have felt a little better to know her decision hadn't been easy, that it had cost her, too. It was a selfish feeling, and he despised it, but it was true anyway. He had felt cast aside, as if he didn't matter to her at all.

"I told you it hurt," she answered, her eyes widening. "I told you it wasn't an easy decision."

He remembered those words, all right, but he also remembered something else. "I didn't believe you. You made it look so easy to just get up and walk away from me that afternoon. Not a tear, not even one look back."

"You thought that was *easy?* Why do you think I had to say all those horrible things? I was taking a hatchet to the ties."

He couldn't tell if she was angry or surprised. Her face didn't give him a clue. After a moment, she just shook her head and murmured, "Wow."

There was no reply to that, so he just leaned forward, resting his elbows on his splayed knees so that she was behind him. Looking at her right now was difficult, between the desire that refused to completely quiet and the feeling that things were somehow going off the rails here. At the very least he had to adjust his memories a bit. At the worst... At the worst she was about to make a life-altering decision under circumstances that weren't the best.

"I'm sorry," Holly said. "I'm a mess and I'm making things messier."

He looked over his shoulder. "Stop apologizing. What mess?"

"I'm mixed-up," she said. "Everything's suddenly all mixed-up. My aunt, my job, what happened to me last year, you... It's all roiling together and I can't sort it out. It's not fair to dump all of this on you."

"I don't feel dumped on." He really didn't. Confused, yes. A little worried, definitely. Mostly for her. Come what may, he had this ranch and all that entailed. If she started doing things like quitting her job, she might wind up with nothing that mattered to her.

He wished he knew how best to help her out, but he suspected that in the end she was going to have to make her own decisions about everything. Well, she would.

She'd been making her own decisions for a long time. There was only one thing he could think of to say.

"Just don't decide anything right now," he said. "Not with so much turmoil. If nothing else, there's plenty of time."

"Not really," she said quietly. "I fly back in less than two weeks."

"Why should that be a deadline? You'd have to go back to give notice regardless, so nothing about your job needs deciding this instant. If you're really thinking about a camp for kids, that's going to take a lot of time and planning. As for me…I shouldn't even be part of this. I'm here, planted like a tree, I'm not going anywhere and you have more important things to deal with, like your grief over Martha."

"God, I miss her. I could almost hate that house, because it's so empty without her. Then I remember the good times."

"That's important."

"Yeah." She fell quiet.

He studied his hands as if they might have some answers when in truth all they wanted to do was reach for her. He folded them together and wondered how Holly managed to turn him into that young man who had spent an entire summer following her around like a buck in rut. He should be feeling stupid right now.

Instead he was feeling like a bull that had scented a cow in heat one pasture over, with a fence in the way. It should have been laughable.

"Cliff?"

"Yeah?"

"Remember how we'd ride out to that stream and sit on that flat rock?"

Boy, did he remember. He'd bring a blanket, she'd

sit in his lap and there in the soft summer breeze, surrounded by running water, beneath the tree-dappled sunlight, he would open her like a treasure, touching, undressing, taking his time until he couldn't stand it anymore, which usually hadn't been very long. Desire had always seemed to overwhelm them almost between one breath and the next. Fast. Furious. He could still hear her cries and moans of pleasure echoing in his head.

"Yeah," he managed to say, his voice rough.

"I wish I could sit on your lap like that again."

"Why?" he asked, barely managing to get the word out.

"Because I felt so good there. I felt like I belonged there."

Right now she didn't feel as though she belonged anywhere, he thought. Not in her aunt's house, not in her job, not anywhere.

But hold her in his lap like that again? He'd suffer the tortures of the damned.

Still, her plea tore at him, and much as he'd been trying to be friendly without getting himself in a position to be wounded again, there was no escaping the fact that he wanted to help her in some way. She was going through a rough time and she was all alone out here. She'd never been here long enough to make friends with anyone except him and Martha. A stranger in a strange land, grieving and alone unless he was willing to put himself out there and take a bit of a risk.

Hell, he was no chicken.

So he slid onto the floor, sat cross-legged and reached back for her hand. She came willingly enough until she sat in the cradle of his legs, her back against him, her head resting beneath his chin.

"Those were good times," she whispered.

"The best." He'd never deny that. He wrapped his arms gently around her. "Close your eyes and remember how good you felt on those days."

She startled him by playfully slapping his arm. "If I start remembering how good that felt, we're going to be doing more than sitting here."

A surprised laugh escaped him, and he gave her a squeeze. "Okay, then think of something less inflammatory."

"With you?" She giggled then sighed. "It was a wonderful summer, Cliff. I wish it could have gone on forever. But it wouldn't have, even if I hadn't left."

"I know. Reality and all that. And while I was miserable for a while, I know that you would have been even more miserable if you hadn't pursued your own goals. Giving up something that big…well, it probably would have poisoned us. You'd have resented giving up your dreams, and I'd have resented your resentment. Not a good mix."

"Maybe so." She wiggled deeper into his lap, just as she had done so often all those years ago. He figured it was unconscious on her part, and he hoped like hell she couldn't feel how hard he was for her. She didn't say anything and didn't move, so he sat there suspended between heaven and hell with her warm rump against his groin.

In an instant he flashed back in time. They were on the rock, she lying on the blanket while he knelt at her feet. Her blouse was open, her bra riding up around her neck, revealing beautiful, full breasts with pink areolas and large puckered nipples. Nipples that had welcomed his mouth and drawn groans from her. Her narrow waist, her gently curved hips, the thatch of dark hair at the apex of her thighs…

He felt as if he were caught in a blacksmith's fire. He remembered joking that she had to stop wearing boots because they were a pain. The giggle that escaped her then died as he at last yanked them away along with her pants. Then he had slid up over her, his own jeans still twisted around his knees, and pressed his face to her honeyed womanhood. How she had groaned and arched into him, gripping his head…

He didn't want this moment, this memory, to end. Alarm bells sounded, because it was going to end, but he didn't heed them. "How about we go riding tomorrow?"

"I'd really love that. But don't you have to work?"

"The work is never done. But I can take a few hours for fun. Essential to sanity and all that."

"I should be working harder on Martha's house."

"Doing what?" He tensed, sensing another rejection in the offing. Probably a wise one, but it was awakening unhappy feelings.

"Whatever odds and ends there are. I haven't donated her clothes yet, for one thing. I just pulled everything out of the closets and drawers to make room for Lisa. I need to go through papers and see if there's any business that needs attending. Sort through things that I don't want to keep…."

"You know, a lot of it can wait. That house isn't going anywhere. I'll help you with the papers if you want. Martha was pretty open about her affairs, and I used to take her bills to town for her, so I've got a fairly good idea of where she stands there. Regardless, you can take a few hours."

Then he waited. He could almost hear her mental

wheels spinning, and he wondered what concerned her most: Martha's affairs or spending a few hours riding together like they'd used to.

"I'd love to go riding," she finally said decisively. "When?"

"Tomorrow morning. About nine. I should have things under control for the day by then. All the lambing is done, so no worries there."

"Can I see the lambs sometime?"

"Absolutely."

Again she fell into a silence that left him wondering. He itched to turn her and take her down on the floor, to press his full length to her, to run his hands over every inch of her, the way he had once done. He gave himself a mental slap and corralled his thoughts yet again. Being with her, he thought with private amusement, was testing his willpower to the extreme. Ten years ago he hadn't needed any, but now he needed it all and then some.

"Cliff?"

"Hmm?"

"Why do you think Lisa came back? I know what she said, but do you really believe it?"

"Well, she's between marriages. That much I know. And with her that may be the whole story, just looking for a better marital bet."

"So you don't think she might have come back here for you?"

Everything inside him suddenly froze. Icicles seemed to drip through him. "The way we parted? She couldn't possibly think I'd be interested."

"It's been six years, didn't you say?"

"About that, but not even Lisa could be that dim. Her moving over to your place and making you miserable would hardly seem like the right move in that direction." But he vividly remembered the way she had tried to vamp him when she first arrived. Really? Did Lisa think he was that gullible?

"Moving over to my place and making me miserable might be her way of getting you to take her back, just to get her out of my hair. Then once she's here she could turn all sweet."

It wasn't beyond imagining. She'd been sweet as could be once...until she got the wedding ring. "No, that's too Machiavellian for her."

"Well, then, maybe she just decided I was a threat so she moved in with me to control things. I don't know. The whole thing is just plain weird."

"I'll grant you that." But Holly had him thinking now. It *was* odd that Lisa would turn to him claiming homelessness for the next couple of weeks. And that she'd tried to vamp him at the outset. "I need to think about this. There's no question that she's manipulative. Maybe she's learned some new tricks."

"Or she isn't as good at manipulation as she thinks."

A laugh escaped him, even as his insides churned at the thought that that woman might be trying to find a way to get around his armor. God, the idea made his skin crawl.

"Why don't you stay in the guest room tonight?" he said. "I don't want to take you back over there, not with her there."

"I'll survive. But I don't want to give her any ammunition by staying here tonight. She's not a very pleasant person, and I may not remain pleasant for long if she starts implying things."

He could understand that. "You probably look at her and wonder how I could ever have married her."

"No, I've seen that kind of transformation before. You've got the person who is all sweet in order to get what they want, and then when they've got it they turn into monsters. Sometimes not right away. They're smart enough to build up slowly, hoping they don't lose anything in the process. But sooner or later they let it out."

"Yeah. Like I told you, I married one woman and woke up with another. It took a few months, but..." He shrugged. "It's done. Just let me know if she gets intolerable. I'll get her out of there."

"I should never have let her have a room," Holly admitted. "It's just that...well, I've done it before. Usually abused women with children who had no place to go for a night. I leap before I look sometimes."

"A kind heart is nothing to apologize for."

A few minutes later she asked him to take her home. He'd have felt a whole lot better if she'd been going back to a house occupied by nothing but the ghost of Martha.

Chapter Seven

Mercifully, Lisa had not put in another appearance last night. Holly had still had trouble sleeping, wrestling with her own mixed-up desires, all of them complicated by the time she had spent with Cliff. Sitting on his lap had felt like a dream come true, a need so deep that she hadn't realized how much she had been missing it all this time.

It had brought back other memories, too, of what it had felt like to lie naked with him under the sky, surrounded by nature, free of inhibition. The way the breeze had felt on secret parts of her that hadn't ever been exposed that way. The slightly tickly sensation as it had ruffled the curls between her thighs. The huge aching sensation when his hot mouth had followed it, teaching her that pleasure could approach pain. The way she had spent most of the summer in a half-orgasmic state, constant anticipation of the next time, the next moment, the next touch. Riding a horse had transformed from a delight to a promise of pleasure. With every movement in the saddle the ache had deepened.

Damn, she had had it bad. And to judge by what she had felt tonight, she still had it bad.

Was that behind her urge to cut out on her job? Or was she just worn-out? And could she be truly serious about throwing away all she had worked for? Had she reached that point?

It was possible. She knew plenty of social workers who simply couldn't do the kind of work she was doing anymore. They moved to desk jobs. They moved to doing social work in other settings, where the emotional strain wasn't as overwhelming. Anywhere but the streets and the impoverished kids who grew up with the sounds of gunfire and the violence they could hear through paper-thin walls, even if it wasn't happening within their own homes.

It took a toll. Maybe eight years was enough. Maybe she had reached the point where she wasn't helping as much as a fresher person might. How would she know?

But morning came, dripping sunshine everywhere, with a sky as blue as an unflawed sapphire. She dressed eagerly, excited about riding with Cliff in an hour. It had been so long since she'd ridden a horse, not since her last time with Cliff, in fact. She loved riding, and that summer, with Cliff, it had become both magical and sensual.

She headed downstairs with some minor trepidation, wondering how Lisa would greet her and whether she'd be a little more pleasant this morning. Much to her relief, there was no Lisa in sight. She found a note on the table.

Gone to town for some shopping. Back in a few hours. Don't lock me out. L

Really? She couldn't afford a place to stay but had gone shopping? Well, maybe she needed some shampoo or feminine products. Something essential. As Holly remembered, there wasn't a whole lot to shop for in Conard City anyway. And hadn't Cliff mentioned that Lisa went on shopping trips to Denver? That would take more than a couple of hours.

Regardless, it was enough she could have her breakfast in peace, enjoy anticipating the ride with Cliff and maybe try to sort through some of her internal confusion.

It had occurred to her somewhere between waking and sleeping that building some kind of youth ranch or camp here might be the perfect compromise for her. If she really had grown reluctant to go back, then she needed to find another way to contribute, one that wouldn't feel like a cop-out. The idea energized her, and had from the moment Cliff had mentioned it, so that was a good thing. Whether she could bring it to fruition remained to be seen, but she doubted she would have time to work on getting a camp rolling once she was back at her job.

Excitement carried her outside once more, however. She had made a thermos of coffee for them to take along, but she knew from experience Cliff would arrive with saddlebags full of food and drink from Jean. She needed to make a point of going over there just to spend some time visiting with Jean.

Standing there, looking around the space she still had, envisioning the bunkhouses, the kids, the garden, all of it, lifted her spirits the rest of the way. Martha would approve and she would enjoy it. So would the kids. It was time to stop thinking about it and talk to someone who could clarify the task so that she'd know where to begin. Somehow she suspected building the bunkhouses would be the very last thing on the list.

She turned around, taking in the vista, feeling the peace of the prairie and mountains settling over her. Something about these wide-open spaces suffused her with a calm it was impossible to feel at home in the city. She wasn't going to blame the city for that, though. No, it was something deep within her that seemed to be answered by the endless vista, the infinity of the blue sky, the gentle whisper of the morning breeze.

Martha could have deeded this place to Cliff, but she hadn't. Maybe her aunt had guessed how much she needed these spaces. She wouldn't put anything past her aunt. She'd learned over the years how canny Martha could be. She never pushed for anything, she never criticized anyone, but when she saw a need she found a way to do something about it.

Here at the base of the mountains, the prairie rolled gently. She saw Cliff appear at the top of one of those small slopes astride his mount and leading a horse for her. She lifted her hand and waved and suddenly felt twenty again.

He answered the way he always had, lifting the cowboy hat from his head and waving it in a wide arc.

Time rolled back ten years in an instant. She ran toward him as she had done all those years ago, her heart lightening with sheer gladness. By the time she opened the gate for him, Cliff was only a few feet away and smiling broadly.

"It's a beautiful morning," he said.

"It most certainly is. I've got a thermos of coffee for us."

"Jean loaded me up as usual. Are you warm enough? Then grab the coffee and let's go. I feel like I'm on a prison break."

The laugh that escaped her was as carefree as any she'd given voice to in a long, long time. Everything seemed to have fallen away except Cliff, the horses and the beautiful day.

She mounted without help, although she realized certain muscles weren't quite what they used to be, and soon they were letting the horses pick their lazy way along.

"No Lisa?" he asked.

"She left a note that she'd gone shopping and I should leave the house unlocked for her if I went out."

"Did you?"

She glanced at him. "Heck, no."

He tipped back his head and laughed, and once again the years seemed to vanish. There had been so much laughter that summer. So much fun, so many tender moments. He was right; regardless of how it had ended, it was an experience to be treasured.

She urged her mount to a slightly faster pace. She wasn't ready yet to attempt a gallop, but she wanted to be moving, away from the house, away from everything. Seconds later Cliff caught up and rode beside her. He shifted his reins to his other hand and reached out to clasp hers. Now they rode so closely together that their knees brushed occasionally.

Just as they had back then. She felt a moment of resistance, fear of opening an old can of worms all over again, then ignored it. The time limit was set, and he knew it as well as she did. This was just a chance to have fun.

And she was so ready for fun. It wasn't long, though,

before Cliff encouraged her to slow down. "I bet you haven't been riding recently. You don't want to get saddle sore."

He had a good point, but she still sighed as she reined in. "It's been ten years," she admitted. Since she had last seen him, but she didn't want to go there.

"All the more reason to take it easy. So do you want to go to the creek or somewhere else?"

The creek, of course. She didn't know why that flat rock had come to mean so much more than most of the other places they had visited. Hell, they'd made love everywhere, from a barn loft to the bed of his truck to an open field and a cave in the mountain. But somehow that place stuck with her—the sound of the water, the overarching trees that had made it feel as if they were in a room provided by nature. And the rock. She'd always loved big boulders and rocks.

"Did I ever tell you about my thing for big rocks?" she asked. "How much I love them?"

"I guess that tells me where we're going." He flashed a smile her way. "You mentioned it. How else would I know that you like them?"

"I think they're beautiful, but I could never put it in words as to why. They just grab my attention, maybe even my imagination. Sounds silly, I guess. It's not as if they do anything but sit there."

"Maybe that's what gets to us, their endurance."

He released her hand as the horses pulled farther apart, needing to pick their own way over the uneven ground. She tossed her head, drinking the beauty of the chilly morning and the bright greens that had begun to emerge from winter. Most of all she savored the sense of freedom that came over her, cutting her free of the detritus of the past, temporarily removing her from her grief for Martha. All of that would return soon enough. For now, just as she had ten years ago, she embraced an experience out of time, an experience so far removed from the burdens of reality that it felt like a sojourn in Eden.

"I've missed this!"

He glanced at her, his turquoise eyes smiling. "So have I."

The phrase seemed so weighted with the desires of the past that uneasiness touched her briefly. Was she making a mistake? But truthfully, she was past caring. So many things had begun to trouble her since Martha's passing that she couldn't deny herself this break. She needed it.

So she gave herself up to every relaxing and exhilarating moment. Going back to the rock could be a big mistake. It might also prove to be the answer to questions she had evaded for ten years. It might even help her, by its endurance and peace, to sort through the mess she seemed to have been falling into since Martha's death.

A half hour later, they arrived at the creek. Towering trees arched over it, leaves feathering out in stunning contrast to the deep green of pines farther up the slope. The creek itself rushed happily, filled with meltwater that had been steadily journeying down from the peaks as the seasons changed.

It was every bit as magical and beautiful as she had remembered it.

The last time she had been here, in early August, the stream had been shrunken, still lively but nothing like the rush and bubble she saw now. She wondered if they were going to be able to reach the flat rock in the middle when the stepping stones they had used before were under water.

Cliff had no such qualms. He just led her to a point
where the bank was gentle and guided them down it on
horseback. The horses didn't seem to mind at all. They
picked their way carefully, but brought them to the huge
flat rock that seemed to have patiently awaited their return for all these years.

"You dismount onto the rock," Cliff said. "I'll hand
you the picnic things Jean sent, then take the horses
back to dry ground."

"But you'll get wet," she protested, even as she
swung down and found stable footing.

"I can dry out. The horses can't stand in this water
for long. It can't be much above freezing."

She accepted the carefully wrapped bundles and a
blanket from him and put them in the center of the
rock, well away from the creek's splashing. When she
turned, he had already tethered the horses within sight
and was sitting on the bank, pulling off his boots and
socks. Then he rolled up his jeans to his knees, probably a useless gesture, she thought with amusement.

Holding his boots and socks under one arm, he
stepped into the water and let out a yelp she could hear
even over the rush of the creek.

She laughed.

"Yup, it's cold," he called. She watched him pick his
way as carefully as the horses had, holding her breath
once when he nearly lost his balance. Then he stepped
onto the rock, spread his arms and said, "Voilà!"

She laughed again.

"Am I good or what?" he asked, a twinkle in his
amazing eyes.

"You're good," she acknowledged.

"I knew you'd agree." He dropped his boots and

reached for the blanket. Together they spread it out, then sat.

Propping herself on her hands, Holly leaned back and looked up at the fantastic canopy growing over their heads. "I think this is my favorite place in the world."

"Then stay."

He couldn't have said anything better calculated to dash the moment. She sat upright and looked at him. "Cliff…"

He held up a hand. "I get it. You're going back. You're doing important work. You'll be leaving and that's that. But I keep wondering."

"Wondering what?"

"Why the hell you can't just do good work here. I mentioned bringing your kids out here. I bet you've thrown up a million mental roadblocks. Hell, you were talking about how this might make it more difficult for them to go home. Maybe you're right. On the other hand…"

When he didn't complete the thought, her initial stubbornness faded. And that had been the real basis of her reaction: stubbornness. Nobody told her what to do except at work. She made her own decisions, her own plans.

She tore her gaze from him and looked up at the trees again. On the other hand, there could be more than one road to the same end. She *was* getting burned-out. She was running from something so hard that she was in danger of making herself ill.

Maybe blaming it on that attack last year was just an easy excuse, a way to conceal something else in her that was dying.

Sighing, she closed her eyes and let her head fall to her chest.

"I'm sorry," he said. "I didn't mean to ruin this for you. It just seems to me that you're burning your candle at both ends, and the woman who came back here for a funeral has burned to a mere stub of what she used to be."

"Why should you care?" she asked wearily.

"Maybe for old times' sake. Maybe because I just care. I'm worried about you, Holly. I've been trying to ignore it, telling myself it's none of my business. You made that clear a long time ago. But seeing the way you were on our ride out here, and comparing it to the woman you've been since you got back here... Holly, you need *something* more than your job. I don't know what it is. I just know in my gut that you're killing yourself."

The old stubbornness tried to rear up, tried to tell her she could do anything she put her mind to, but since coming here she had begun to realize that wasn't true. She had limits just like every other person in the world. Physical limits, emotional limits.

Her friends at work, Carla and Laurie and Sharon, had been trying to tell her that for the last few months. Rotate, they kept telling her. They could see what Cliff was seeing, too, and given how close they were to her, it was even more surprising that they'd noticed it. He, after all, was seeing her after an absence of ten years. They saw her every day, and the contrast shouldn't have been as obvious to them.

Unless it was so blatantly true that the whole world could see it.

She lowered her head again, listening to the voice of the rushing creek, seeking some kind of answer within herself. Did she just need a vacation? Did she need to take a break from the streets? Or did she need a major life change?

That latter idea scared her half to death. Yet wasn't that exactly what she was considering by thinking about a youth ranch here?

Maybe that scared her as much as anything. Not just the change, but the size of the task. She couldn't imagine where to even begin. She'd need advice from all kinds of professionals at the very start, and she wasn't even sure which ones. A lawyer? Probably. Psychologists, probably. And then what? What steps in which order?

"I don't know how to start," she mumbled.

"I'm sorry?"

She lifted her head, feeling the fear and hollowness that must be showing on her face. "I don't know how to start. Where to begin. I'd need so much help, there'd be so many hurdles. I'd need people who'd actually be willing to work with the kids when they come here. How can I afford that?"

"I don't know about affording, but you might find plenty of volunteers."

"Who?"

"Me, for starters. I could help you build what you need. I could teach kids about animal husbandry. Jean would probably love to teach gardening. Then we've got a whole slew of good teachers here, both at the community college and in the public schools. I bet they'd be willing to volunteer time to help. But that's not the immediate issue. Is it?"

No, it wasn't, she admitted to herself. There was the whole part about jumping off a cliff into the unknown. The possibility of having it all blow up in her face. "What if it doesn't work?"

"Then I'd be very surprised if you couldn't get another job just like the one you already have."

He had a point. What with budget cutbacks, jobs weren't as available as they once had been, but on the other hand a lot of people quit for the very same reason she was facing: burnout. So there were always new openings, and finding an experienced social worker wasn't easy. When most quit, they quit the streets for good.

"Do you think it would work?" she asked finally.

"Well, I'm not the biggest authority on youth ranches for inner-city kids, but I'd be surprised if there aren't enough needy kids in *this* state to keep you going."

She hadn't thought about that, either. It didn't just have to be inner-city kids.

"Do you know," she said slowly, "that one of the reasons poor kids don't do as well in school is because they don't enjoy enrichment opportunities over school breaks?"

"Really?"

She nodded. "It's like the spigot gets turned off during the breaks, and when they come back they have to make up lost ground, unlike the children of better-off families, who get to the library or visit museums or take trips. It's like their learning turns off every summer. But once they get back up to speed, they do every bit as well. And when there are summer enrichment programs, they never lose ground at all. We've been working on that, but funding is hard to come by."

"So you'd give them summer experiences that would help them keep up?"

"That would be part of it, along with taking them out of danger for a while."

"I think you'd find a lot of teachers around here who'd want to help with that. Want me to ask around?"

"Not yet," she said finally. "I haven't even figured out the first steps. I probably need a complete plan. And somewhere along the way I'll need licensing. But for now, I've got to figure it all out. Who it would serve and how."

She released the last of her resistance, and tried to envision the complete life change she'd only been playing with so far. Had this been what Martha had meant about finding her dream? It was possible.

Apparently he decided they had been serious long enough. He sat up straighter and said, "I don't know about you, but I'm starving. I had breakfast before sunup. If you haven't noticed, the sun is rising awfully early these days."

His change of subject came as such a relief that she giggled. "I didn't notice."

"Slugabed," he teased. "Jean filled me up before the crack of dawn."

"Then what happened?"

"I helped my hired men start the worming and the vitamin shots."

"You have to give vitamins?"

"You saw my range. Do you really think I'd have healthy, plump animals if I didn't supplement from time to time?"

"I wouldn't know," she admitted. "I feel kind of stupid."

"Why?"

"Because I never bothered to learn much about what you do."

He waggled his eyebrows at her. "I seem to remember we were busy with other stuff."

She felt her cheeks heat and hoped he couldn't see. Even though the trees weren't completely leafed out yet, they did cast the world in a greenish glow.

She accepted half a ham sandwich from him and bit into it, savoring it. "Great ham!"

She also noticed his bare feet. That long-ago summer she had told him he had beautiful feet for a man. He still did. They were masculine, for sure, but narrow and well formed with high arches. More than once she had made him moan with pleasure by giving him a foot massage. He had always reciprocated, too, teaching her that nothing could relax her as fast or deeply as having her feet massaged.

She missed that.

She squirmed as she realized there was a whole lot more she missed, as well. Like being able to reach out and touch him at any time, in any way she chose. Like seeing that look come into his eyes that meant they were about to find a private place to make love.

She giggled unexpectedly as a memory returned.

"What?" he asked.

"The person who thought that making love in a hayloft would be romantic never tried it."

A laugh escaped him. "That wasn't one of our better ideas, even with a blanket."

"A horsehair blanket!" she reminded him. "That was almost as bad as the hay."

"Hey, it was the only one handy."

"I don't know what was worse, the stink or the itch."

The shared laughter filled her with warmth, relaxing her utterly. It was good.

And there was only one way it could be better. She quickly looked away as laughter faded and resumed nibbling at her sandwich. She'd had cereal for breakfast, but it seemed to have moved on, and despite the relatively early hour, she felt ravenous.

Crossing his legs, Cliff dove into the contents of the bags and came up with a leafy green salad to go with the sandwiches, some warming bottles of soda and a small plastic container of cupcakes. "A feast," he said. He held up a couple of sporks, making her laugh again. "I'm more in the mood for coffee than soda, though."

She passed him the vacuum bottle she'd carried. It had a double cup and he filled them both with steaming brew, passing her one.

A bridge had been crossed, she realized. They had moved beyond all the lingering tension left by that summer and were growing comfortable again. Only now did she understand how much she had missed that. Missed him.

Oh, yes, she had ached when she left him. Months had passed before she could stop thinking about him almost constantly.

But the weirdest thing was that now she was sitting here wondering why she had insisted on breaking it off with him. She'd been full of youthful idealism and determination, sure she couldn't be content being a ranch wife for the rest of her days, but in the process of making those decisions she had cut herself off from other possibilities and a number of wonderful things.

She put her sandwich down on the wax paper, wrapped her arms around her legs and rested her chin on her knees, staring up along the rushing, swollen creek, thinking about the way choices rushed by in much the same way, often with unintended consequences. Choices that couldn't be recalled.

Cliff, seeking to pursue his own life, had married the wrong woman. She had married no one. She'd dated a few times, but if she was honest with herself, no one had measured up to Cliff.

"It couldn't have been any different." She spoke the words aloud, musingly, then wished she hadn't. That was going to open up a whole bunch of questions she wasn't sure she could answer.

Seconds ticked by before he said, "Us breaking up, you mean?"

"Yeah. I guess."

He surprised her. "I don't think it could have."

She turned her head, resting her cheek on her knees. "Why?"

"You're asking me? And damn, I wish you'd eat more."

"I will." She waited, wondering if he was going to answer her.

He had started his second sandwich, but put it down and reached for coffee. "We were too young and we were pulling in different directions. You needed to go places, I needed to stay here. Hell, my family has been planted here since 1878, and how likely do you think I was to abandon the homestead? I couldn't."

"Certainly not with your mother ailing. How is she, by the way? I wish I could have met her."

"Nobody saw much of her back then. She couldn't get out of bed. She's doing okay. She and Dad have settled in New Mexico where the weather is warmer year-round and she cuts quite a swath in her motorized cart. Her multiple sclerosis hasn't worsened any. Maybe it's even improved."

"I'm glad they're okay."

"So am I. Anyway, I couldn't leave. You know that, even if I didn't tell you all the reasons. Primarily I needed to make this ranch run so that I could help them out, as well as support a family of my own. I couldn't just pack and leave, Holly."

"I understood that."

"Not saying you didn't. But you *had* to leave. Nothing of what you wanted was here."

"Except," she admitted quietly, "you."

He nodded. "I felt the same about you."

She hesitated, feeling her heart hammer with trepidation, but deciding it was high time she told him the truth. Hell, she should have had the guts to do it years ago, but back then she'd been too chicken to face up to herself. "I'm sorry I was so hard on you. God, I took an ax to you, to everything. I was horrid."

"No kidding."

She squeezed her eyes shut, feeling the rebirth of an old pain.

"You had to be cruel," he said after a moment.

With difficulty she forced her eyes open. "No, I didn't."

"Yes, you did. I was arguing with you, objecting to everything you said, fighting to keep you, which would have been about as good as caging you. You had to ax it. You made me so mad I started to hate you, which I needed. And you made sure you burned the bridge completely so you'd have no further contact with me. I get it. You deliberately left us with no way back."

She averted her face, looking up the stream again, thinking life was like that water, rushing by, here and then gone. Nothing to cling to. Her throat tightened, and her eyes burned. "I was still awful."

"I don't think there was another way to do it, so stop beating yourself up. At that time, there was no other way to go. You set us both free to do what we needed."

"It didn't feel a whole lot like freedom."

"No," he agreed. "It felt more like desperation. Anyway, I was furious with you for a long time. I'm not sure I ever really got over it until lately, but it eased, and eventually I could even see the justice in what you'd done."

"I'm not sure it was justice."

"It was at least right. Damn it." He threw out an arm. "We had an idyll. It wasn't reality, for the most part. Two crazy kids locked in a haunting and fantastic summer romance. But then like everyone else on the planet, we had to face reality. We were headed down different roads. End of story."

She nodded, unable to find her voice around the lump in her throat. He had described it perfectly, just the way she thought of it, as a summer idyll without a future.

But how often had she wished she could recapture those halcyon days, however briefly. They couldn't build an entire lifetime, but they could sure as hell make up a beautiful experience. Nor did she feel that she wanted this story to end again.

She watched him move the food out of the way. Then he reached out and gently unclasped her arms, easing her back on the rock. He leaned over her, his head framed by the trees and sky.

"It was perfect," he said, brushing her hair back behind her ear. "Absolutely perfect. Perfection is a rare and priceless thing. You don't find it often, and it seldom lasts. We were blessed."

She tried to swallow the lump, then asked, "Are you measuring everything else against it?"

He shook his head. "No."

"I think I have."

Despite the fact that his face was in shadow, she saw his eyes widen. "Oh, damn, Holly, no."

He scooped her into his arms and rolled over so that she lay on him, not the hard rock, then he caught her face between his hands and kissed her. Hard. The way he had once kissed her when the flame between them seared them with passion. She opened her mouth to him, wanting that kiss as much as anything she had ever wanted, well aware that this was dangerous, that they were still headed along their separate roads. If ever the universe had decreed that a relationship wasn't meant to be, this was it.

But she was helpless before the force of her longing and need. For some reason she needed him now, more than ever, but in different ways she could scarcely put a name to.

His hands began to wander, first stroking her back, then slipping between them until he held her breasts. It was so familiar, yet as new as the moment. The hunger within her strengthened, driving everything else away except awareness of him beneath her and the magic his hands worked. It was as if she had been made only for him. She deepened her kiss and lifted her arms until she dug her fingers into his shoulders, silently begging for more. Her entire body tingled and ached, and the throb between her thighs intensified, promising heaven. Her hips rocked against him, and she felt his hardness rise up to meet her.

It would be so easy, so right, and it would answer every craving she felt.

He startled her by tearing his mouth from hers. He pulled his hands from her breasts and cradled her face once again. "What's changed?" he asked.

She felt almost sideswiped by the sudden shift in mood. It took a few seconds for his question to reach her.

The way he said it left her wondering what he meant: Was he speaking to her or to himself? "Changed?"

"Holly, I still want you every bit as much as I ever did."

She closed her eyes. "Me, too," she admitted, wondering if her heart might hammer its way right out of her chest. She was pressed to him so intimately now, her breasts against his chest, her legs splayed to either side of his, leaving her feeling at once open and eager. She had never, ever stopped wanting him.

"So what's changed?" he asked again. "We're lying here striking matches in a bed of pine needles, if you get my drift. Do we really want the forest fire? Has anything changed that much? You're leaving in less than two weeks."

She couldn't argue the truth of that. "One way or another, I have to go back. I still have a job."

"Exactly. So do we want to play with this kind of fire again if nothing has changed?"

"When did you get so sensible?"

She saw him smile faintly. "I grew up," he answered. "I think you have, too."

"Somewhat, anyway. I know we can't go back. I know we're playing with fire."

"So that leaves the question. What has changed?"

"This time," she said slowly, "I don't want to go back to my job."

"Ah, damn," he said quietly. He released her face and wrapped his arms around her, holding her close. "We can't go back in time. You said it yourself."

"I know."

"So it could be really stupid to set off this conflagration again. We're older now. We need something more. Right?"

"I don't know," she admitted. "I just don't know. I'm so confused about everything."

"Which is a good reason not to strike the matches." She felt him draw a deep breath, but at least he didn't let go of her. He lifted a hand and stroked her hair gently.

"I could make love to you right this minute," he said almost roughly. "I've never forgotten, not an instant of it. Sometimes, when I let my mind wander, I can feel your skin against mine, feel your curves in my palms, remember the way your nipples tasted, the way *you* tasted. I can remember your moans and sighs, and damn, I miss it all. I want it again. But I'm older now and I need more than a couple of weeks. And so do you."

"I can't promise that."

"Neither of us can right now. After ten years we're practically strangers. You're not sure which direction you want to take, and my direction is right here with sheep and goats and the land."

Her head lowered to his shoulder, and she inhaled his unforgettable scent as deeply as she could. He was right. She was more confused than she could ever remember feeling. It would be utterly stupid to light a fire that would burn them both, especially when they both remembered how badly it had burned them last time.

She had to get her head sorted out. She had to pick a path. She had to settle on something internally one way or another. Part of her wanted to stay here, but part of her also recognized her obligations at home. Nor would she be content with a life where she wasn't helping children.

So that left a choice between Chicago and trying to build that youth ranch here. The ranch would be a huge undertaking, and while the idea excited her, it daunted her, as well.

"I miss Martha," she said against his shoulder. "She had more common sense in one finger than I'll ever have."

"I'm not sure that's true. In a lot of ways, you're very much like her. She just had more years of experience. But if she were here, what would you ask her?"

"Which way to turn."

"You know what she'd say."

"To make up my own mind. I know." Holly sighed, then couldn't prevent herself from nuzzling him. She turned her head until her nose touched the skin of his neck, slightly stubbled just below his jawline. He smelled so good. Just taking that aroma into her lungs swept her back to that long-ago summer.

"Holly..." His tone was somewhere between a warning and a groan.

This wasn't good, she thought. It would be so easy to slip into the past, to feel so young again, so free, so heedless. But she wasn't that person any longer and neither was he. And that was the danger. To try to relive that summer, no matter how wonderful, would be folly, and whatever came from it wouldn't be based in the reality of now.

She lifted her head, propped herself on her elbows and looked down at him. His turquoise eyes looked almost smoky and were half-closed. He held very still, as if he feared a movement might push them over the edge. It might. That would not be wise.

But she rested as she was, savoring the close contact with him, realizing just how much she had missed lying with him this way, feeling his hard angles and planes against her softer curves. Not as soft as they had been back then, but still soft compared to him.

"I missed you," she admitted quietly. "Sometimes I

missed you so much I ached and wondered if I'd been a fool."

He didn't answer, leaving her to wonder if he'd moved from love to hate in an instant. Even though he said that he now understood, she wondered how long that understanding had taken him. How long it had been before he could forgive her for the awful things she had said, deriding him and his choices in life as going nowhere and doing nothing important.

Cruel, hateful things that she still had trouble believing had emerged from her own mouth, things that remained etched in her brain as if with acid. She could hear herself and wanted to cringe.

It had been necessary? That was an awfully generous thing for him to say. Maybe it had been. But the person she hoped she was, the person she wanted to be, wouldn't have attacked him that way. She would have found a kinder way to sever the knot that had bound them over the summer, gentler words to explain that she had a different path to follow.

Except even now she wondered if it would have worked. She'd been open all summer about how she was going back to school and into social work. Never had she once wavered in her determination. Even that hadn't prevented him from falling in love with her.

Or her with him, if she was honest. What else could have caused her all those tears, all that pain, after returning to school?

For all these years, they had avoided each other. He'd never come over to see Martha when Holly was visiting, and she didn't think that was an accident. She hadn't dropped by to find out how he was doing, nor had she asked Martha, who had seemed to figure out quickly that all mention of Cliff was off-limits.

She had built a bubble, then a wall around that summer. She had even eventually shut down her memories of it as much as possible, refusing to entertain them at all.

So what had she given up, and what had she gained? Damned if she knew anymore, but she'd been utterly certain back then.

She pushed herself up a little, brushed a light kiss on that mouth she had once known so intimately, and rolled off him, staring up into tree boughs that seemed to brush the blue sky.

It was time to answer some questions. To make some decisions. To commit, one way or another, either to returning permanently to Chicago, or to trying to build her youth camp here. That decision could not be based on Cliff. It had to be her own. Otherwise she could make herself miserable, and possibly him. They both deserved better.

"It's odd," she remarked.

"What is?"

"How different things look now than they did back then. That summer with you, well, that was a time and place all its own. And all the times I came back to visit Martha, I came for her. I thought this was a peaceful place, but I couldn't see anything else here. I couldn't see how beautiful it is. I just saw emptiness. Nothing to do."

"Boredom?"

"Not exactly. Just…emptiness. I'm used to a pretty hectic kind of life, and there were times I thought I'd suffocate in the quiet out here."

"Some people do feel that way," he agreed. "We've got a movie theater the community had to buy to keep it open. One movie a month, sometimes two. We've got socials, if you're into that, barbecues, parades, and even roadhouses if you like country dancing and want a beer. A real hotbed of entertainment."

"I wasn't thinking of entertainment, exactly. I was thinking more off the wide-open space. Sometimes it felt so empty it seemed oppressive."

"Funny," he drawled, "I feel oppressed when I go to the city. Shut in."

She gave a little laugh and rolled over on her side to take a playful swipe at his shoulder. "You know what I mean."

His smile faded. "No, actually I don't. What are you trying to say?"

"I've changed," she said carefully. Some things were so hard to put into words. "I don't see emptiness here anymore. I see how beautiful it is. I even see possibilities. Like the youth-ranch idea. It seems overwhelming, but I think I could do it."

"I'm sure you could. What you've done already seems pretty impressive to me. You need to talk to your psychologist friend, and then to a lawyer to find out what's required at the minimum. Once you've got a clearer picture, you might feel less overwhelmed."

"You're probably right. At the moment, I feel like I don't even know where to begin." She reached out to rest her hand on his shoulder.

He sat up immediately, and she felt almost offended. But then he said, "Let's finish eating. And let's not strike any matches."

She had to remind herself that he had just told her he still wanted her as much as ever, and that he'd given her a passionate kiss, before she could settle down enough to eat.

He was protecting her, she realized. Protecting both

of them. Remembering the young man she had once known, who had been far more impulsive, she was impressed by how he had grown. She wondered if she had matured as much herself.

Certainly she was not the same person she had been back then. Her ideals had taken a bit of battering, and her view of human nature wasn't quite as nice as before, but in what ways had she grown? She supposed that therein lay at least a part of the puzzle she was trying to solve.

She managed to finish the sandwich and some of the salad. By the time she stopped, she felt overly full, which gave her some idea of how little she had been eating. Twenty pounds in a year wasn't worrisome, but it had gotten to the point that even her doctor had told her she needed to put some weight back on. Imagine hearing that from a doctor. She was more used to hearing that she could do to shed five or ten pounds.

The stubborn five or ten that never wanted to go away no matter what. Well, they were gone now.

And maybe some other things were gone with them. A certain innocence had fled a long time ago. A sense of safety…well, her job had been chipping away at that pretty steadily, she guessed. Those guys on the street had just completed the change.

"Holly?"

She tilted her face toward him. "Hmm?"

"Why did you say you don't want to go back? Burnout? Fear? The attack?"

It was a fair question, so she gave him a fair answer. "I'm working on that. It's a bit of everything, I guess. For some time now I've been wondering how effective I really am."

"Why?"

"Because most of the time I don't know. Cases come, cases go. People move. Other caseworkers take over if the situation changes to something they're better trained for. I spend a lot of time wondering how much difference I'm really making. You could say I'm operating on faith that what I do makes a real difference. Occasionally I get to see that difference, but that's rare. A lot of problems are intractable."

He nodded, encouraging her.

"So I don't get much of a sense of accomplishment. All these years are catching up with me, I guess. I'm starting to feel hopeless, and that's not helpful to anyone. Then since the attack..."

"Just don't tell me again how lucky you were."

"But I was. A lot of people live like that. I just dipped my toes into it during my workday. Until I was attacked. Then I was well and truly *in* what these people are dealing with. Anyway, I still don't feel safe on the streets. I went for a long time thinking that everybody in the neighborhood knew I was a social worker, and that put me in a kind of protective bubble. The worst the troublemakers ever did was make offensive comments when they saw me, but they left me alone. Then I discovered that bubble was of my own imagining."

She looked down and realized she was twisting her hands together. "I don't want to be a chicken. So it's all messed up. I despair sometimes, I feel overwhelmed sometimes, I'm not sure how much good I'm doing and I'm afraid now."

"Being afraid is sensible. Don't think you're a chicken. That attack was what, a year ago? You kept going on those streets. That's not a chicken."

"Maybe not. But it makes it all more difficult. I don't stay late as often as I used to, so I'm sure that's cut my effectiveness. It's just a whole mess I need to work through. But out here... Out here I see a different way to help. If I do it right, it could be so great."

"I'm sure it could. I need to take you over to see Cowboy."

"Cowboy?"

"It's what he goes by. Years ago he and his wife bought a ranch and they take in foster kids, lots of them. Some they've even adopted. It's working for them. Maybe they'll have some ideas."

"I'd like that."

"It may have to wait until your next trip out here. I'll check, but I think they just left on a big family camping trip. They do it every year when school lets out."

Man, that sounded good to her. Closing her eyes, she could easily imagine having some of her kids out here—heck, any kids—and showing them these kinds of joys. Tall grasses, big spaces, animals... Her eyes popped open. "What if I wanted my kids to ride horses? I'm not sure I could take care of them in addition to everything else."

He chuckled. "What are neighbors for? I'm sure we could arrange trail rides for the kids. If things really go well and you have lots of kids, we'll deal with the horse issue. One thing at a time."

"You're right. I'm jumping the gun. There's so much else I need to take care of first. It might take a few years to get to the point of worrying about horses."

"I don't think you're jumping the gun," he said quietly. "I think you're getting excited about the possibilities. You need that excitement, Holly, and you sure didn't have any of it when you got here."

No, she hadn't, and it wasn't just because she'd lost her aunt. Once she'd had excitement for her job. Then it had slowly seeped away. As difficult as it was to face, she had to be honest with herself. She no longer felt fulfilled by what she was doing. She no longer woke to each day raring to go. Far from it.

All of a sudden, Cliff stirred and looked at his watch. "Damn, we've got to go back. The vet's coming out today to vaccinate the lambs and kids. I need to be there."

She helped him pack up, then watched him go get the horses and bring them out to the rock. Taking care that she didn't have to get her toes wet. How many men did she know who were that solicitous?

As they were riding back, he asked, "Wanna take in a movie tonight with me? Given that we don't get the new releases here, it might be something you've already seen."

"I see so few movies that's highly unlikely. I'd love to go." Dating a man she had kissed off ten years ago. How likely was that?

"Great. I wonder how angry Lisa is at being locked out."

Holly couldn't restrain a laugh. "I guess I'll find out."

"I could come to the house with you. I don't have to leave you at the fence."

"Why borrow trouble? I'll deal with her."

At that moment she felt she could deal with anything. A great weight had seemed to lift from her as she faced her job dissatisfaction, almost as if she had made up her mind about what she was going to do. And she had a movie date with Cliff.

Lisa seemed like a small blip on a very big radar.

Chapter Eight

At the fence, she dismounted and passed the reins to Cliff. "It's been wonderful."

"Yes, it has. Thanks." His smile was warm. A smile she had never thought to see from him again. "Call me if Lisa turns into a handful. I'll pick you up around five and we can have a bite at Maude's before the movie."

"I'd like that."

He tipped his hat and began to ride away with her mount in tow. Now all she had to do was head back and face the Lisa music. The woman's sports car was sitting in the drive, somehow managing to look ominous.

When she rounded the house, she found Lisa sitting on the porch swing looking majorly annoyed.

"Have fun?" Lisa asked acidly.

"Yes, thanks," Holly replied pleasantly. Reaching into her pocket, she pulled out the key and unlocked the front door.

"I told you to leave the house unlocked," Lisa said. "I've been sitting out here forever."

Holly let that pass. Even if Lisa had returned just after Cliff and Holly rode off, their entire trip hadn't quite taken three hours. "Sorry," Holly said. "I'm a city girl. I don't leave anything unlocked."

"Then you'll have to make me a key to use, if you're going to do this often."

"No, I won't make you a key. Sorry, but you'll only be here until I go back to Chicago. I guess we need to plan better."

Lisa followed her into the house and into the kitchen, where Holly started a pot of coffee. "You're not very nice."

For some reason those words clicked with Holly. She finished preparing the coffeepot, turned it on, then faced Lisa.

"You're right, I'm not being very nice. Have a seat and join me for some coffee." There was a gleam in Lisa's eyes, a smugness in her expression that Holly could read too well. She'd seen it countless times when a child tried to guilt-trip her or someone else. It occurred to her that Lisa was acting more like a child, and showing very little real skill at manipulation.

When the coffee was ready, she brought two mugs to the table, along with a growing curiosity. She sat facing Lisa. "So what's really going on, Lisa?"

"I don't know what you mean."

"I think you do. You came to your ex looking for a place to stay. Most women wouldn't do that. Then you came here hoping my aunt would put you up for a while because a few days with Cliff wasn't enough. Why not? Do you really have a job in Glenwood Springs?"

Lisa scowled. "Yes, I do. But it doesn't start until

the end of the month. And I really can't afford to rent a place yet."

"I believe you. But that's not the whole picture."

"What do you mean?"

"You come here looking for help but you're nasty to everyone. I'm sure you've heard that you catch more flies with honey than vinegar. I know you can be nice enough, because Cliff wouldn't have married you otherwise. So what's eating you right now? Why are you treating me this way when I gave you a place to stay?"

Lisa glared at her. "What is this? Five-cent therapy? I don't need that stuff."

"Maybe not. I'm not a therapist anyway. I'm just wondering why you can't even be nice to someone who is helping you. What are you afraid of?"

"What the hell makes you think I'm afraid of anything?"

"You," Holly answered simply. "You remind me of barbed wire. That amount of fencing is designed to keep something in or keep something out."

Then she rose with her coffee and went to sit on the porch. It was a beautiful afternoon, a great time to laze here and envision the life she would really like to have. Plus, she had a date tonight with Cliff. Only time would tell if that might be a mistake, but right now she didn't care. Pieces inside her were shifting around, forming a new picture, and she was liking what she was seeing.

At some point she dozed off, into vague but happy dreams. She was wakened by the sound of steps on the porch. With effort, she opened her eyes, realized it was getting later, and then saw Lisa sitting on a nearby chair.

"I'm sorry," Lisa said. "You're right. I'm pretty angry."

"About what?" Holly stifled a yawn and tried to sit

up straighter. Her coffee had long since grown cold, but she drank it anyway.

"A lot of stuff. Most recently it's the jerk I was married to until the divorce became final last month. He cheated on me, then blamed me for it."

Holly nodded. "Did he knock you around?"

"Some." Lisa fisted her hands. "Thing is, I hit back. So when I left you know what happened? I didn't get to take anything. Nothing at all. Didn't matter that I worked, too. No. A woman doesn't hit back, I guess."

"I'm sorry."

"I'm glad to be out of there. But that doesn't mean I have to be happy. So all I have is a little bit of my own money that he didn't spend because I made it on my own after I left, and a job waiting for me, and nothing in between."

"What about family?"

"There was just my dad. He's been gone for three years now. Funny, he told me not to marry the jerk in Gillette. One of the last things he said to me. I should have listened, because the creep spent my inheritance money, too." She shrugged. "Well, I spent some of it. I'm not good with money. Cliff probably told you that."

Holly kept mum. "We don't talk about you." *Much,* she amended silently.

"Anyway, I guess I was spoiled growing up. Jean sure seemed to think so. I caused Cliff problems, and I admit it. I was stupid enough not to get what he was trying to tell me. I'd never had to worry about money before, and sometimes I thought he was just being mean. Maybe he was, but he was no kind of mean like the guy I just divorced."

"You've had a rough time."

"My dad also used to say that we make our own

beds." She sighed. "Anyway, don't get the idea I'm going to change or anything. I'm angry most of the time, and I don't see any reason to stop being angry until things get better, okay? But I'll try to be politer. I think I can do that."

"It would help," Holly agreed cautiously. She wondered how much of this was true, and how much of it was an excuse. In a way it sounded too damn pat. There was something missing here.

Two thoughts occurred to her, and neither of them was something she could ask Lisa: that her father had abused her in some way, and that he had used money as a means of control and punishment.

It would sure explain a lot, but she figured she would never know. It seemed like a good time to change the subject.

"I'm going out tonight for dinner and a movie," she announced, wondering what kind of trouble that might bring. "With Cliff."

"So you're the next victim?"

Victim? The word astonished Holly. "Why would I be a victim?"

"You know I was married to him. Big mistake."

"Why?"

"He was a whole lot of fun at first, when we were dating, and even for a while after we got married. Then it got so he was working all the time, and he claimed money was tight, so we couldn't go anywhere anymore. I started to feel like a prisoner, so I took off on my own. Then he said I was spending more than he could afford. He put me on an allowance and got upset when I over-drafted. It turned into hell."

Holly considered a cautious answer. "Ranchers have to work hard. And most are just scraping by."

"And Jean hated me. You know who Jean is? She nagged me about doing stuff. But she's the housekeeper, right? It's *her* job. I was hoping she'd get mad enough to quit, then we could get someone who'd do the job right. That was stupid, too, I guess. Cliff cared more about her than me."

This was certainly an interesting rendering, Holly thought. She'd have expected this kind of viewpoint from someone much younger and less experienced. Like maybe twelve or even fourteen. Certainly not a grown woman.

She looked out over the prairie, watching grasses blow in the warm afternoon breeze, and thought about it. "How old were you when you married Cliff?"

"Nineteen."

"What was the rush?"

"My dad was a control freak. I wanted to get away. I didn't know I was marrying another one."

"You've had a rough time," Holly remarked. The picture she was forming wasn't a happy one for Lisa. She felt the first inklings of real sympathy for the woman. And while she didn't know the exact pieces in play here, she was developing the definite impression that this woman-child had been arrested in her development in some ways. How or why she could only speculate. "So good things are waiting for you in Glenwood?"

"I hope so. I've got a job at a salon there. I'll be doing hair and teaching courses in makeup. I'm good at it."

Holly nodded. Looking at Lisa, she could well believe it. "But they can't take you on right away?"

"Someone is leaving. I'll be taking over. But not until the end of the month."

"That really puts you in a bind."

"It sure does. Actually, I'm glad you said I could stay

here. I don't know if I could have handled even a few days in the same house with Jean. She *really* doesn't like me. How well do you know Cliff?"

"I met him ten years ago," Holly said cautiously. "But this is the first time I've seen him since."

"Well, take it from me, all work and no play makes Cliff a very dull boy. Being stuck on that ranch was like being in prison. The only fun thing was riding. I miss riding."

But not Cliff, evidently. "Well, I'll only be here a little longer," Holly said briskly.

"Yeah, I guess you're safe. You have a life to go back to."

Which indicated that Lisa had not. She'd been fleeing her father and fell into exactly the wrong arms, at least for her.

Holly glanced at her watch. "I need to get ready. Cliff will be here soon. There's food in the fridge."

For once Lisa contented herself with a simple, "Thanks."

Cliff picked her up a few minutes after five. He'd spiffed up a bit, wearing new jeans and a carefully pressed white shirt. She almost felt grungy in comparison. Her jeans were well-worn and her lightweight sweater had come from the rack at a Goodwill store. It showed some wear.

But his smile was warm, and his eyes passed over her appreciatively, making her feel as if he'd drizzled hot honey over her. Her insides clenched in response.

"You look great," he said as he helped her into the truck.

Holly half expected Lisa to poke her head out and say something, but the woman kept out of sight. Interesting. Maybe they'd found a bit of peaceful ground on which to meet.

As they were driving away, Cliff asked, "How much hell did Lisa give you?"

"Not much, actually. I think we came to at least a minor meeting of minds."

"Congratulations. What happened?"

"Did she ever mention her father to you?"

"Not much. I gathered she had a tense relationship with him. She didn't like to talk to him."

"Well, from what she said, she married you to get away from him."

After a few seconds, he gave a low whistle. "That might explain a lot."

"It might. Anyway, she announced she's angry and doesn't intend to stop being angry until things get better, but she'll make an effort to be polite with me."

"I can applaud that." He flashed her a smile that quickly faded.

"What's wrong?" she finally asked when he remained silent.

"I was just thinking. I spent a whole lot of time wondering where I went wrong with Lisa. It takes two to make a mess."

"It's easier to make one when one person is in the relationship for all the wrong reasons. She picked you for an escape hatch. The problem was, it wasn't really the kind of escape she wanted. Anyway, I wasn't there, I'm not going to judge or even comment, except to say she still has some growing up to do. And you shouldn't be too hard on yourself. I think it was doomed from the start."

"Maybe so. The hole just kept getting deeper."

She looked out the window at the passing countryside. The days were getting longer as the solstice approached, and she liked the fact that the late afternoon was still bright. She supposed that her return, and now Lisa's, had given Cliff a lot to think about, and she suspected not all of it was good.

After all, he'd ultimately been rejected by two women, and basically for the same reason, whether he realized it or not. She'd had bigger things to do than be a ranch wife, and Lisa had seen the ranch as a prison. If he put that together, he was apt to give up all hope of marriage and family.

Yet here he was, only a few days after he'd initially greeted her with such dislike, taking her out for dinner and a movie. By any measure, that made him a truly big man.

"How'd it go with the vet today?" she asked. High time she showed some interest in his life.

"Pretty good. They all seem healthy. We have to do some eyedrops on some of the lambs and kids. We started vaccinations and should finish tomorrow, but all's good."

"Okay, how do you get eyedrops in those animals?"

He laughed. "With great difficulty. The mamas don't like us handling the babies, and the babies don't like the eyedrops. We get a whole lot of caterwauling, I can tell you. And sometimes it takes three of us to get it done."

"Do the moms attack you?"

"They would if they could, but we separate them out. That's when the trouble begins. But overall, it's not too hard. Just sweaty. We get them into a holding pen one at a time and get it done as fast as we can."

"How do you tell who you've done?"

"That's why they invented washable spray paint. We just put a big X on them."

"Do you brand?"

"Ear tags."

"Oh, that must be fun, too."

He laughed. "Oh, yeah. Before you leave, you need to come over and meet my kids."

She joined his laughter. "That's a cute way to put it."

Holly had been to Maude's diner only a few times that long-ago summer, with Cliff. Aunt Martha had preferred to do her own cooking and viewed dining out as frivolous. After meeting Maude, as crusty a curmudgeon as ever walked the planet, Holly had privately wondered if the two women just couldn't get along, or if her aunt really was dead set against going to restaurants.

Maude was still there, hardly changed by a decade, and joined by one of her daughters, Mavis, who could have been a younger clone in both appearance and demeanor. Menus got slapped down like a dueling challenge, glares accompanied the taking of orders and it was a wonder coffee mugs didn't crack the way they got slammed down.

Holly had trouble keeping a straight face. If she hadn't known that this was typical service here, she could easily have been offended. Locals, however, were used to it, and Maude was a great cook.

Conversation lagged, though. Holly wondered what was bothering Cliff, as he was usually a chatty enough companion. Was he thinking about his marriage to Lisa? Linking it, perhaps, to the reasons she had left him? God, she hoped not. People changed, and the changes she was going through might lead her right back here.

But what made her think he would want her? Oh, she apparently still aroused his passions, just as he aroused hers. He'd made no secret of that. But what if he didn't want her in any other way? She couldn't blame him for that. They had a past, and in the end it hadn't been good. Especially for him. He hadn't spoken one cruel word to her, but she'd spat her share of them at him.

She had cut the cords that bound them all those years ago, and she'd been merciless. Ranching was a dead end. Yes, she'd said that. She needed to do *important* stuff with her life. Right.

She squirmed on the bench seat and wondered who that woman had been who had spoken such cruel things. She remembered feeling desperate, but that was still no excuse. A man had asked her to marry him, had told her he loved her, and that was how she'd responded?

God, she wished she could take an eraser to her brain and utterly wipe away all those harsh words. She was as guilty as Lisa of wounding him.

He certainly didn't deserve it. He'd been kind to her back then, and was being kind now, except for his initial reaction to her. He worked hard, he was building a future, he was performing an important job. Where would the world be if everyone felt they were too good to raise sheep and goats?

She sighed and gave up on eating. The salad she had ordered was too big, too full of grilled chicken. She should have ordered the dressing on the side, because while it was delicious, Maude was as generous with it as she was with everything else she served. She could almost feel her arteries clogging.

"Something wrong?" Cliff asked.

"No. Yes. I don't know. I was just thinking that you've had rotten luck with women. First me, then Lisa. You didn't deserve any of it from either of us."

To her surprise, when she dared to raise her gaze, a smile hovered around his mouth. A devilish twinkle

resided in his amazing eyes. "Who said I've been un-
lucky with all women?"

She felt her eyes widen, then she burst into a laugh.
"Score."

He laughed with her. But as his laughter died, he
said, "Just forget it, Holly. You did what you needed
to, and while I felt scalded, I survived. We were a lot
younger then. Who's to say you were wrong? What's
more, if you'd been kinder, I might have been harder
to shake. At that point in time, you needed to shake
me. I seem to remember I didn't make it easy on you
to say no."

"You're being awfully kind."

"I'm being awfully realistic. I've been through a marriage with an unhappy wife. I'm glad I didn't share one
with you."

He had a point there, she admitted.

"Anyway," he went on, "we keep belaboring this. It
was the wrong time, if nothing else. I wasn't going to
stop you from finishing college, not even if you'd said
yes. I should have been smart enough to realize that it
couldn't work. Not then. You'd finish college, you'd take
your master's and then what? Throw all that work away
to come back here? Not likely. I wasn't using my brains
and I know it. So let's just let go of it, okay? You've got
a future you're trying to work out right now. That's what
matters. And me, I'm still firmly rooted right here to the
land. I'll help you if I can, whatever you decide, but I'm
still going to be me, and you're still going to be you."

Her heart plummeted a bit as his words hit home. She
supposed she ought to be glad he'd found such a kind
way to essentially tell her it wasn't any more likely to
work now than it had been a decade ago.

So that's what he'd been thinking about, she thought

as they went to the movie. He'd been thinking about the fire they'd been so close to igniting that morning, and he had decided it probably wasn't a good thing for a lot of reasons. Nothing could grow between them, nothing permanent, anyway.

Amazing how bad that made her feel, especially when she remembered how unhappy and annoyed she'd been to see him when she arrived here. Worse to realize he was probably right. But that old tug was still there, the one that had drawn her to him in the first place and made it so hard to leave him.

Maybe the smart thing would be to light that fire, get it out of their systems. There was a darn good chance it wouldn't be as good as they remembered it, especially since they were older now and ruled less by hormones.

Just have the sex for old times' sake, clear the table of the constant yearning, get rid of the need for restraint, then see what happened. It might clear the air rather than making it murkier.

She was quite sure she had never had a stupider idea.

"Wanna go dancing?" Cliff asked after the movie.

Holly was tempted, but she also knew she was walking a fine line between giving in to her desire for Cliff and trying to keep them both unscathed. Have a fling? Look how well that had worked ten years ago.

"I don't think so," she answered, even though it would have been fun to do some line dancing, especially with him. "I've still got so much to do at Martha's."

"Yours now," he reminded her. "If you need any help, you'll let me know?"

"Sure. Thanks."

The closer they got to their houses, the darker and emptier the road grew, until several miles passed without sign of another vehicle. Of course, this was ranch country, full of early risers, most of whom were probably tucked into bed or about ready to land there.

The sky was full of stars, and Holly commented on them. "You don't see stars like this in town. In Chicago, I can only see a few. I've practically forgotten what the Milky Way looks like."

"Well, we can remedy that," he answered.

A short way down the road, he turned onto what looked like a wagon track, and jolted them down it a ways. When he stopped and parked, Holly suddenly felt very young again, much as she had the first time they had parked like this. Anticipation began to fill her, but she stepped down on it, trying to ignore the way her body wanted to wake up.

"Come on," he said.

They both climbed out and he spread a blanket in the bed of his truck. He opened the tailgate and gave her a quick boost. Soon they were lying side by side, looking up at a sky so full of stars that it was hard for her to believe it was the same sky she saw every night at home in the city.

"It's breathtaking," she said. "So many, many stars. And the Milky Way is so clear and obvious."

"When you see it out here, you can understand why so many ancients, and even some modern people, believe the dark spot is the womb of creation."

Indeed she could. It took little imagination to see that it resembled female genitalia. In fact, the resemblance was quite striking.

She sighed. "I've heard the legends and stories. But you have to see it like this to understand it. Didn't the Egyptians think the Nile was a reflection of it?"

"I've heard that, but don't ask me what an ancient Egyptian believed. You're the one with the education."

That stung her, and for a moment she forgot the stars. "Does that bother you?"

"I know enough to do what I do. I read a little more out of interest. But I sure as hell don't have any degrees."

"So?" At that she pushed up on her elbow. "Tell me that's not bothering you. Why should it? You're successful at what you do. What brought this on?"

"I don't know," he admitted. "I don't usually think about it."

"Well, stop it, then. I happen to think you're a pretty smart guy."

He laughed and just as she dropped onto her back to resume her study of the sky, he rolled up and leaned over her.

Everything inside her seemed to still in a hush of breathless expectation.

"Holly?"

She could barely make a questioning sound.

"I can't stand it. We either get you home now or I'm going to make love to you, consequences be damned. I'm going to light that match."

She caught her breath, then reached up and cupped his cheek, feeling as if her muscles had become spaghetti. "Is that why you've been so quiet?"

"It's getting to be all I'm thinking about. I want you and I want you every bit as much as I ever did."

"A one-night stand?"

"If that's what you want."

She wasn't sure that was what she wanted, but hadn't she been thinking that this might clear the table? Who the hell cared, anyway? There was nothing, absolutely nothing, she wanted as much as she wanted Cliff right then.

Seeing him leaning over her, a shadow framed by the infinity of sparkling stars, drove away all reason. She couldn't be sensible for another minute.

She slipped her hand from his cheek to his neck and pulled him toward her in an answer as ancient as the stars above.

Cliff had wanted to be sensible. Hell, he'd been trying since he'd gotten past his first irritation at seeing her again. In fact, he suspected that most of his irritation had arisen from realizing he was far from over her.

But his memories were memories, and the present was the present, and he knew how foolhardy it would be to believe that anything of the past still survived. They were different people now.

But the desire had survived. Oh, it had survived, and no rational argument or thought had been able to squash it. One-night stand? If that's what she wanted. Maybe it would set him free of her spell.

Because never, not once, in his life had he felt a desire as deep and wild as the one Holly awoke in him.

He'd known the instant that he'd pulled off the road that he was going to make love to her. He *had* to. It was either that or go insane. He was giving short shrift to everything at the ranch because he couldn't stop this pounding need from dominating his thoughts. Even Jean had finally said, "If you want the girl, go for her." How often did Jean offer comments on his love life? Once that he could remember, and that had been her threat to leave.

He must have been stomping around like a bull who smelled a cow in heat in the next pasture.

Then all attempt at thought vanished as his mouth met Holly's. As warm and sweet as ever, tasting slightly of the popcorn they'd eaten at the movie, but still recognizably the taste of Holly. He had never forgotten her taste, her scents, and now he knew he had never forgotten the way her lips moved beneath his, the little sigh that escaped her as she parted them and granted him entry.

Familiar, so familiar, yet as exhilarating as the first time. His heartbeat thundered in his ears, his body tensed and clenched in time with it, his groin grew heavy and ached.

He wanted to move slowly, to savor every single instant of what might well be the last time forever, but when her hands clawed at his back and she tore her mouth from his to groan his name, he lost his last restraint.

Rearing up, he tugged at her sweater. She ripped at his shirt.

The spring night was chilly and getting chillier. He felt the cold air raise goose bumps but he didn't care. All he could think was it was a damn shame the night was so dark. He could barely make her out, but memory recalled the size and shape of her breasts, the rosy pink of her nipples and areolas. When his hand cupped her, the feeling was at once so sensual and so familiar.

In an instant past and present slammed together and fused. That long-ago summer, they had been so eager in their lovemaking, impatient, filled with laughter, always in a hurry because later there would be another time. It was only after they were sated that they would linger over one another, lazily, gently, beginning to build the anticipation again.

He wanted to linger over her this time, but that

thought was swiftly lost in need, and she was coming right along with him. He bent his head, sucking her nipple into his mouth, tormenting her with the lash of his tongue. She was already swollen for him, but his ministrations made her nipple grow larger and her groans grow deeper. Her nails dug into his back, urging him on. Her hips bucked up, her legs separating and winding around him.

It was going to be exactly like that long-ago summer. Except he couldn't remember reaching this peak of hunger with her before. It was as if ten years had merely built the desire to nuclear proportions.

The jeans had to go. He had just enough sanity left to pull a condom out of his pocket before he yanked the denim off both of them. Kneeling between her legs, he ripped open the packet. She grabbed it from him, pulled out the condom and rolled it on him. The shaft of hunger speared him so intensely he thought it might kill him. He ached in every cell for her, for completion.

She pulled him down. She didn't want to wait. So many things he wanted to do to her, all lost in a driving, overwhelming need. He lifted her knees, then dove into her. She twined her legs around his waist, opening herself fully.

They knew this path, one traveled many times before. But never before had it seemed so intense.

Almost before he knew it, they exploded together, soaring to the stars overhead and shattering into a million flaming pieces.

He wanted to never return.

Cold. It was the first sensation to penetrate Holly's awareness after a climax so intense everything inside her had seemed to freeze in the moment of satisfaction.

She had hovered there, as never before, held on its rainbow and denied for so long the return to earth.

She could feel Cliff withdraw, too soon, but necessary. In the dark she couldn't see what he did with the condom, but suddenly his hands were there, trying to help pull her clothes back on.

She stopped him. "Not yet," she whispered, her voice barely louder than the rustling grasses that surrounded them. She ignored the night's chill, a minor inconvenience, and levered herself up on one elbow, pushing him onto his back.

He didn't argue. She wished she could see him better, but this was the darkest night she could ever remember. So her hands had to do all the work, drinking him in. She traced his contours, from his strong jaw down his neck, then lower.

It was like taking a well-remembered, well-loved journey, relearning his planes and hollows, the firmness of muscle over bone. She could feel the magic building again, the passion like a phoenix rising from hot ashes. Her touches were featherlight at first, but as she felt him quiver beneath each one, they grew firmer.

She rediscovered his small nipples, and bent to suck them and then give him a nip. The groan that escaped him filled her with a heady sense of power. He was all hers, for now, and that fueled her own desire, pumping it higher until she could barely hear anything but the drumbeat of her blood.

She trailed her mouth lower, caressing his hard belly with her lips, teasing him gently with her tongue, tracing patterns on him that she knew must feel cold as soon as her tongue passed.

He moaned again and his hand grabbed at her shoulder, as if he needed to feel that she was real. He didn't push her or direct her, just hung on to her.

Man, did she understand that feeling. Then she reached the nest of tight curls between his legs, smelled his musky aroma mingled with hers. Control was slipping away from her again, but she clung to it desperately.

His staff was hard again, already, and her first brush against it caused it to jump. The invitation was clear. She lowered her lips to it, running her tongue along its length, then at last taking him inside her mouth.

He called her name, his hand on her shoulder tightening until his grip was almost painful. She showed him no mercy, taunting and teasing him until he quivered from head to foot. Finally, with a sharp jerk, he erupted.

Then, astonishing her, almost before the ripples of completion had finished running through him, he shoved her back and settled himself between her thighs. Gentle fingers brushed at her most tender flesh. She gasped as she felt him part her petals, as the cold air touched her where it seldom did, and then the heat of his mouth settled over that tight knot of nerves, a sensation so good it hurt.

She wanted it to go on forever, but the intensity was shattering her, and there was no way to slow her climb to the pinnacle. Riding the lash of his tongue, she soared upward at dizzying speed until finally, inevitably, she tipped over the brink and drifted like embers back to earth.

This time she didn't stop him when he reached for their clothes. This time the cold penetrated the magic. Not a word passed between them until, at last, covered again, boots back on, they lay together in the bed of the truck with the glories of the heavens wheeling over them.

He wrapped her snugly in his arms, tucking her head onto his shoulder, throwing his legs over hers. He even managed to pull part of the blanket over her.

"Too fast," he murmured finally.

"We were always fast." With her head pillowed comfortably, she looked up at the stars and wondered what it all meant.

"Yeah," he said. "Like rockets. Once the fuse was lit, there was no stopping the launch."

A soft laugh escaped her. "I guess that hasn't changed."

"I wish I could change it. I'd love to spend time lingering over you, but tonight is not going to be it. Too damn cold."

"Hey, I thought it was fantastic!"

"We were always fantastic."

In this way at least, she thought, but didn't say it. They'd lit the fire he'd warned about earlier, and she had discovered that it was all still there: the need, the nearly furious pace of their passion—none of it had declined. But there had been some other feeling there this time, and as she tried to tease it out, she worried about what it might be. She had thought casually about having a quick fling to settle this, but she felt nothing had been settled. Far from it. The entire past had risen up, reminding her what she had walked away from so long ago.

And part of her knew that walking away again was going to be even harder. Why? She couldn't say.

All she kept thinking, and feeling, was that the years hadn't quieted anything at all. Maybe they'd even fueled it more.

A shiver passed through her before she could prevent it.

"We need to get you home," he said. "Before you turn into an icicle."

"I'd forgotten how cold it gets at night."

"We're not really into summer yet. You can still almost smell snow on the breeze some nights."

A good description, she thought. Her body didn't want to move. She didn't want to leave his embrace. She wanted to stay just like this. But reality once again played the trump card as she shivered again.

"Let's go home," he repeated.

Home? That caused her to walk down another corridor of reflection as he helped her out of the truck bed and into the cab. Where was home now? She shivered a few more times until the engine warmed up enough to blast some heat at her. Silence had again fallen between them, and she wished she knew what he was thinking. That this had been a mistake?

Maybe it had been, but she wouldn't take it back. She had to make up her mind about some things, and quickly, she decided. No more playing around with a vague future. She had to nail it down. So where was home now? In Chicago? When she had arrived here, she'd been utterly certain she would return to her work there. Now she wasn't so sure.

Another door had opened, and she needed to decide if she would walk through it. Even if she did, however, there was no guarantee that she would ever have more from Cliff than episodes like the one they had just shared.

She could move here and they could become neighbors. He might even help her with her project. But he might not want one more thing from her.

Could she live with that? Could she live without it?

She had thought making love would clear the table.

Instead it had left her more mixed-up than ever, feeling like a dandelion puff adrift on the breeze. Where would she land?

She honestly didn't know.

Chapter Nine

The next days were busy and weird all at the same time. Far from being underfoot, Lisa drove out each morning and didn't come back until late afternoon. Holly couldn't imagine how she was occupying herself.

Clint didn't come by or even call. That troubled her, and while she realized he was probably seeking some necessary space after what had happened, she couldn't help but feel a little hurt. She understood it, it was probably wise, but to make love like that, then disappear off the face of the earth?

Then she remembered he had said something about needing to start vaccinations on his lambs and kids. Maybe that was keeping him busy. How the hell would she know?

She thought about calling him, but instead forced herself to attend other things. She spent a whole lot of time out walking the property, trying to envision what she would do with it. The walking stilled her thoughts and gave her some clarity, at least about that.

She laundered and organized her aunt's clothes for charity. She went through all the papers in her aunt's desk, trying to figure out what mattered and what didn't. She put the photos she found into an envelope to place in an album later. It was surprising, however, to realize that after all the generations that had lived in this house, after Martha had spent her entire life here, there was so little detritus. Martha had kept her footprint small, all right. There was really nothing to get rid of, nothing to throw out. The house approached sterility.

She wondered if Martha had planned that, or if that was just the way she had lived. She cried when she thought about it, cried a few times because she couldn't just sit down with her aunt and have one last chat about things. Anything.

Cliff.

He haunted her thoughts and she wished she had someone to talk to about him. Not that anyone was going to be able to untangle the mess inside her. No, she had created that mess, had been creating it steadily since she came back here. Now she had to deal with all the knots herself.

She told herself to stop thinking about him. She created a to-do list for her youth ranch idea and started with the lawyer, Carstairs, asking him to look into all the legal and liability angles. She couldn't take a single step without knowing that much.

Then she called her friend Sharon back in Chicago.

"You're thinking about doing what?" Sharon practically shrieked the words.

Holly repeated herself.

"I think that's a fabulous idea! How soon do you need me?"

Mixed-up as she was feeling, Holly still laughed. "Hold your horses there, girl. I haven't even found out what the legal aspects are yet. I'm mainly worried that if I don't do this right, I might not really help the kids."

"What in the world is wrong with you?"

"Well, taking them out of their environment and showing them something better and less frightening is great. But having to put them back..."

"Ah. You think it might be harder for them when they come home."

"It could be. I don't want to do that to them."

"Well, if you want my internationally recognized opinion, it all depends on what you do. A lot of places offer opportunities to disadvantaged kids. You wouldn't be the first or only, and it seems to work well. You broaden their horizons, keep them sharp for school and instill confidence." She paused. "These children need confidence, Holly. They get so little from life. You need to show them other opportunities, open new doors for them to walk through. And give them plenty of positive strokes. God knows, they get few enough of them. So when do you need me?"

"Are you serious?"

"As a heart attack. I love the idea. I want to help. I know I'm a city girl, but I used to visit my uncle's farm in Nebraska."

Holly laughed again. "You're on. But I've got to clear a lot of decks and hurdles first. And I'll have to come back to Chicago to clear out things there. I don't want to leave too abruptly. Make the transition smooth for my kids. At this point I don't even know how fast I can act here. It might be pointless to start anything but the legal stuff before next spring."

"Just as long as I'm on your staff. I'll work for my supper and a place to sleep."

The words touched Holly, making her throat tighten. "Thanks."

"I'll bone up on the psychological aspects for you. Now for the important question."

"What's that?"

"Did you meet your rancher again?"

Oh, man, she'd forgotten she had told Sharon about that a few years ago during an evening spent chatting with a bottle of wine nearby. Too much wine? Maybe. She didn't remember getting drunk, but she guessed she had gotten relaxed. "Yes," she said carefully.

Her rancher? She hated realizing that she wished that were true.

"So how was it? Tense? Has he forgiven you? Do you still feel the same?"

"He's nice, it was tense at first, but he's forgiven me and…we're moving on." Kind of a half truth, because she didn't know if anything was moving or where. He'd vanished.

"Is he still a hunk?"

Much as she didn't feel like laughing, she laughed anyway. Count on Sharon to cut straight to the chase. "Yes, he's still a hunk."

"Oh, yum. If you don't want him, maybe I can catch a flight out tomorrow."

Holly knew she was joking. Sharon couldn't afford a plane ticket any more than she could. Buying one every year had stretched her budget to the snapping point. But apart from that, she felt a very uncharacteristic burst of annoyance at the remark.

She had no claim on Cliff, but that didn't keep her from resenting the idea that Sharon might set her cap for him. Damn! Talk about confused.

Sharon was no dummy, though. "I was just kidding," she said after a moment. "I wouldn't do that to you."

"I know," Holly admitted, swallowing her irritation. "Anyway, if there's anything between us, it doesn't seem to be going anywhere." Which was true, especially after the long silence from Cliff. Maybe he had discovered the magic was gone. Hard to believe, considering what she had felt, but he wasn't her, obviously. Or maybe he'd felt that connection between them awakening again and decided that distance was the safest course. "I don't know," she finally said to Sharon. "I poisoned that well a long time ago."

"People change. You said he's forgiven you. So you want my advice, girl? If you want him, go for it."

Easy to say, harder to do, Holly thought when she finally said goodbye.

She was just deciding what to do next when she saw a dusty delivery truck coming up her drive. She hadn't ordered anything. The driver must be lost, and she was probably the last person in this county who'd be good at helping him out.

She stepped on the porch, prepared to offer her phone if necessary, when the guy jumped out the passenger side, carrying a huge cardboard box. "Holly Heflin?" he asked as he mounted the porch steps.

"Yes."

He passed her a handheld computer and stylus. "Sign here."

Moments later he was driving away while she looked at an impossibly big box and wondered what it could contain. She'd have thought Martha had ordered something just before her death, except the box was clearly addressed to her. And she couldn't make hide nor hair of the sender's address.

Shrugging, she picked the box up and carried it inside, where she placed it on the kitchen table. Using a small knife from the drawer, she sliced the tape and opened it.

Foam peanuts in a variety of colors concealed the contents. She hated those peanuts and wished they'd go back to the old days of shredded newspaper. Not that anyone seemed to read a paper newspaper anymore.

Shoving her hand in, she felt another box. She pulled it out carefully without sending peanuts flying. Her heart almost stopped. She knew a florist's box when she saw one. Sympathy flowers? But part of her was hoping for something else.

She quickly cut the green ribbon around the box and the tape holding the lid on both sides. She pulled away the lid and gasped at the spray of long-stemmed red roses. A card peeked out from between the stems and she quickly lifted it.

I know a dozen is traditional, the typed note on the card said. *But this is one for each year. Cliff.*

Ten red roses.

Card in hand, she sat down at the table and let the tears come. She wasn't sure exactly how he'd meant that, but it somehow seemed to open up a part of her heart that she'd been keeping carefully closed. As the door on the past opened the last bit, agonizing pain filled her.

"Oh, God, Martha," she whispered to the empty house. "What did you get me into?"

When she was sure she no longer sounded as though she'd been crying, she called Cliff. Some corner of her mind noticed that the dial tone made a series of quick buzzes before steadying to the usual one, and she wondered vaguely if she was going to have to get someone out to look at it.

Cliff didn't answer his phone, so she left a message, thanking him for the flowers and asking him to drop by when he had time.

She just simply didn't know how to add up the flowers with his absence. He'd been there every day, and now that they had made love, he had disappeared?

She didn't know whether to be angry or hurt. She spent time talking on the phone again with Sharon and Laurie over the next few evenings, and she had one conversation with the lawyer, Carstairs, who told her he thought he could have the legal issues wound up by the end of the summer.

"You being a licensed social worker with a master's degree in Illinois is going to help you here. We can get you licensed, but to approve the ranch idea we're going to need some plans from you. Facilities, activities, the training of the people you'll have helping you. That's going to take longer, obviously, but I know some people around here. I'll check with them. They might know who can help staff your place."

He paused. "Liability might turn out to be the biggest issue. Taking care of other people's children, you know."

She didn't exactly know, but she got the picture.

She'd dealt with various programs back home, and she remembered the kinds of inspections they had needed to pass and continue passing. But liability had been handled by the state and city.

"You know," Carstairs said, "you'd find it a lot easier if you opened a foster home. You might want to talk to Hugh and Anna Gallagher about that. The problem I see here is that you're just one person. It might take you several years to get through all of this. You'll certainly want to think about quitting your job and settling here. You're going to need to be on top of everything."

Well, she had several years. She was still young. As for quitting her job… Damn, she needed to settle one way or another, she supposed. Martha had made certain that she'd never have to work again, if that's what she had wanted and if she was reasonably careful, but this ranch idea…

She had another idea. "What if I bring kids out here with a parent or guardian?"

"Well, that would certainly be a whole lot easier. I could have you set up as a guest ranch in no time at all. Might be a better starting point while you build up."

It might indeed. After she disconnected, she sat staring at the roses in their vase. She'd tucked the card into her purse so Lisa wouldn't see it. The woman had all but disappeared from the landscape, but she still wasn't certain trouble couldn't appear in a flash.

Staring at the roses made her think of Cliff, of course. Was this his way of getting even? Had the note meant that she'd caused him ten years of hell?

It was possible, even if she found it hard to believe of him. Worse, as she sat there looking at the roses, as she wandered outside trying to envision what she wanted to build here, she was wondering more and more why she'd been so damn determined to leave this place behind.

Even now she knew she never would have been happy just being a rancher's wife. Needy kids had been tugging at her all her life. But had she been foolish in giving up what she had with Cliff? Why had she been so certain she couldn't be just as helpful here? There were needy children everywhere, with basically the same challenges. Kids out here might not be living with violent streets, but they could still be hungry, mistreated, abused, struggling to deal with poverty and broken homes. No place had a corner on that.

But for some damn reason, she had been convinced that staying here would be like staying in a cage. Ten years later, she wasn't at all sure about that. Maybe because her work had showed her that there were all kinds of cages.

She walked around the house, thinking that she had only a few more days here, Sharon's words still ringing in her head: "If you want him, go for it."

Apparently he didn't want her. The roses, which at first had touched her so much, were starting to feel like a goodbye. After all, he'd been spending every free moment with her, and now he couldn't even call? A roll in the bed of his pickup truck had evidently been enough to convince him that some things really *did* die. Unfortunately, she had discovered exactly the opposite. After years of ignoring her memories of that long-ago summer, now she couldn't seem to tamp them down.

It *had* always been fast and furious between them. A look, a touch and the explosion had become imminent. She remembered all the times they'd run giggling to find some privacy. Not too difficult out here. They'd made love under the stars, under the sun, under the trees and almost never indoors except that one memorable time in the hayloft. If the water hadn't been so cold in the streams, they'd probably have made love there, too.

Images of him, long forgotten, began to resurface. She sat on the porch swing and closed her eyes, giving them free rein. The way he had looked as he'd risen up out of icy water on a hot day, water sheeting off his gleaming, muscular body, his staff already hard for her. The way he had looked galloping toward her across the pasture after his day's work was done. Once, his hat had gone flying and she'd laughed so hard that she fell in the deep grasses, only to find him hovering over her a minute later, tugging at her clothes, trying to make a bed from their shirts, until the sun kissed every inch of their bodies.

How easy it had all been, from laughter to passion, as if they had been set free of all constraints to play in any manner they chose.

The other night had reminded her of how his hands had felt on her—slightly roughened from work, but always gentle no matter how strong. He knew exactly how to tease her with his mouth and fingers until her breasts swelled and ached for him, until she opened her legs as wide as she could just to feel those featherlight touches of his fingers. Then his mouth on her most private place, sampling and tasting until she lost her mind.

And it always happened so fast. For them foreplay had become afterplay, when, lying in the glow of satiation, they had taken time to touch, look and learn. He had loved the mole on her rump, and never failed to kiss it, claiming it looked almost like a heart. She had retorted that only eyes blinded by passion could see it that way.

She had traced the jagged scar on his back from

when he'd been thrown from a horse as a child and slid down a wooden fence post that had a nail sticking out of it. He had insisted that the tetanus shot had hurt worse than the nail.

She knew his body as well as she knew her own, maybe better. But there had to be more than that, didn't there?

Being like playful puppies for a summer was great, but it wasn't enough for permanence, right? So maybe she hadn't been wrong in her decision to pursue her long-held goals. If she had stayed here, she might have wrecked everything with resentment.

So why was she sitting here and wondering? It had become the road not taken, and there was no way to turn back and try it now. How many times did she need to remind herself? And why did she keep asking the same questions?

He had confused her. Last time she hadn't been confused at all, but now it was different. Older hadn't apparently made her wiser. Or maybe being older had opened her up to a broader range of possibilities.

Not that it mattered. The days were slipping away and he was avoiding her as if she had the plague. Maybe for good reason.

Swinging slowly back and forth, she watched the afternoon shadows lengthen. All she knew for certain was that she had to make up her mind about one thing: the direction she wanted to take her career now. Go back to Chicago, resume her duties and use this place as a vacation house? Rent it out? Or go for the guest ranch and possibly youth ranch?

Until she made up her mind and took action one way or another, nothing at all in her life was going to be settled.

Then everything got settled in one fell swoop. Lisa came back before dinnertime, waved and started to pass her.

"You've been gone a lot," Holly remarked with a smile. "Did you find a job or something?"

"I've been over at Cliff's." Lisa smiled back.

Holly froze as Lisa breezed by. For an instant the pain in her heart was so crushing she couldn't even move. Then anger rose in a tsunami.

Livid would have been a mild description of what Holly felt. She chopped vegetables for dinner as if she were killing them. The knife hit the cutting board with repeated, resounding thwacks.

Cliff hadn't wanted his ex around, but now she was spending all day, every day at his ranch? Feeling used and soiled, Holly tried to change her flight to an earlier day, but couldn't manage it. She was stuck here for another four days. So she took it out on the vegetables with the chef's knife.

Red roses, one for each year? She slammed the knife into a pepper. That was certainly an original way to kiss someone off: with roses. He should have sent dead ones.

Thwack!

Well, she had to give him marks for getting even. All that talk about forgiveness? Ha! If he had been plotting this all along he couldn't have done better. Then after all that stuff about Lisa, he had her over there every single day?

Thwack!

She supposed she deserved it. What she had said to him a decade ago could still make her cringe inside. But whether she'd deserved it or not, he shouldn't have had sex with her.

Because he had just turned something beautiful into something so sleazy she wanted to vomit. She felt more violated than she had after the attack in Chicago.

And *that* she did not deserve.

"I'm going out," Lisa called. "I'll be late coming back."

If she came back, Holly thought without answering. She whacked at an onion.

Well, if she knew one thing for certain now, it was that she was going to leave her job and move here. She was going to sit right under his nose, not give him the satisfaction of driving her off and do her thing with those children, come hell or high water.

He could live with his duplicity now, every single day.

She scraped the veggies into the heating oil to sauté them. She couldn't even remember what she had thought she was making, and she didn't care. As soon as the vegetables were cooked a little, she'd cool them down and shove them in the refrigerator.

She wondered if she would ever have an appetite again.

But she had to keep moving. She couldn't slow down, couldn't sit around. Anger was driving her, and she had to let it out somehow.

After she cleaned up her abortive attempt at dinner, she pulled on her shorts, a T-shirt and her jogging shoes. She hadn't taken a good run in a while, but now she needed one.

She decided to run down the driveway toward the county road. It provided the safest surface and seeing how often her cell phone couldn't get a signal out here, it would be just her luck to step into a prairie-dog hole or something and need an ambulance when no one knew where she was. At least if she stayed on the drive and got into trouble, Lisa would find her eventually.

God, until just a short time ago, she would have thought it impossible for Cliff to be such a creep. She wasn't naive or anything. She'd met some real creeps in the course of her job, but still, she wouldn't have believed Cliff capable of this.

Well, what if he wasn't? a stubborn portion of her mind asked.

But how else could she interpret this? If he'd come over, if he'd even called, it might have removed some of the sting.

Well, maybe not, she admitted with brutal honesty. But at least she wouldn't feel quite so much like discarded trash.

She reached the county road, and by then began to feel a little better. She could handle this, all of this. She wasn't that invested in Cliff. She was more invested in her ideas to bring children out here to experience a whole different look at life. To receive the freedom to grow and explore new opportunities. She had enough money now. She could probably build a couple of small guest cabins and bring families out here for a few weeks at a time. She should probably start with older children, the ones at highest risk. She figured once she explained it back home to her bosses as a scholarship program, they'd probably do their best to make it possible, especially for moms who might lose their benefits if they took a few weeks off from looking for work.

Yeah, she'd find a way. A scholarship program all nicely tied up with a legal bow that would make it possible. She'd just need to get some established charity involved, and she knew more than one that might.

So it would work. She might have the basics ready to go next summer.

And to hell with Cliff anyway.

She heard tires crunching on gravel behind her and eased over to the side. *Probably Lisa coming home early,* she thought. *Must not have found what she wanted.*

But the thrum of the engine quickly told her it wasn't Lisa at all. Reluctantly, she glanced over and saw Cliff looking out the window of his truck.

"Get lost," she said sharply.

"What did I do?"

"You know."

"That's exactly the problem. I don't know. I sent you flowers. I got your message. I've called three times and you haven't called back. If I hadn't been so busy…"

"Busy with Lisa?" she demanded.

"Lisa? What—" He broke off. When he spoke again, his jaw was clenched. "Get in."

"Get lost." She kept running.

"Damn it, Holly."

"Just go away. I'm done with you."

"Really." He jammed on the accelerator then. Flying gravel missed her as he pulled away. When he reached the house, though, he didn't turn around and come back. No, he parked, and she saw him climb the porch steps and take a seat.

Damn it all to hell, she thought viciously, and picked up her pace. He'd messed with her ten years ago, even though he hadn't meant to, but he was messing with her again. This time he *had* to know what he was doing.

Apparently he'd even taken up lying. Called her three times? She hadn't heard the phone ring. When he didn't get an answer, he should have tried again later. Had he?

Evidently not. Three attempts to reach her, even assuming that was true, was hardly enough for six whole days.

She reached the front yard, such as it was, and stood at the foot of the porch, stretching. "I told you to leave."

"Not until we straighten out a few things. Why didn't you call me back?"

"Because you didn't call."

"I sure as hell did. I left messages."

She paused in the process of stretching her hamstring. "Messages?" she said finally. The anger that had been boiling over suddenly turned down to a simmer.

"Messages," he repeated. "You *have* heard of voice mail? We even have it out here in the boonies."

She put her leg down and stretched the other hamstring. "How am I supposed to know I have voice mail?"

"Surely you've heard the beep on the phone." His tone was nearly acid.

She *had* heard a beep, she realized. "How would I know what it is? I use a cell phone all the time at home."

"Oh, hell," he said.

She bent over to touch her toes a few times, then straightened, shaking her arms out. "It doesn't matter anyway. Apparently you've decided you want Lisa back."

"Like hell."

"She's spending all her time over there."

"I don't know what she's been telling you, but…"

"Oh, just give it up, Cliff. I know what's been going on. You got even with me and—"

"Even with you for what?" he demanded. "What the hell kind of person do you think I am?"

At last he stood up and marched to his truck. "Have a great life, Holly. I'm tired of getting blown up in your minefield."

Her minefield? Agape, she watched him gun his engine and tear out of there.

The dust cloud hung in the air for a while before the freshening evening breeze started to carry it away.

She felt like that dust cloud and didn't even know why.

Chapter Ten

Holly couldn't sleep. When Lisa came home in the wee hours, she was still sitting on her bed, with a few folded shirts beside her and an open suitcase. She didn't have to stay here. She could get a room in Denver until it was time to catch her flight to Chicago. She could lock up the house and go, and to hell with Lisa. Let her stay with Cliff.

As she listened to Lisa come up the stairs, though, her chest tightened until she almost couldn't breathe. How many nights that long-ago summer had she come in terribly late from time spent with Cliff? The creaks of the stairs were still familiar and they mocked her.

But Lisa wasn't even trying to be quiet, unlike when Holly had made the same journey. In fact, from the unsteadiness of the steps, she suspected Lisa was drunk.

Drunk and driving. *My God!*

But not even that could shake her out of the painful despair that filled her, nor erase Cliff's final words.

Your minefield. What minefield? He was the one who'd made love to her and then immediately started seeing Lisa again.

God, that hurt. Her sense of rejection had no bottom to it. She had to leave as soon as possible, get away to clear her head and...

And what? In her heart of hearts she knew she wanted to do the youth ranch. It was as if Cliff's passing remark had unlocked a dream she hadn't realized she had. Her soul craved this whole idea, much more than it craved going back to the streets and constantly trying to hold back a flood with a broom.

Because that's how it felt. She often had no way to know how much she had helped, or if her efforts had an enduring effect. People vanishing from her caseload was the only indicator she got. It might mean things had improved. Sometimes it did. Once in a while she saw a child again and heard good news. Equally, it might mean that some child was gone.

Once they moved out of the system or into a different part of the system, she fell out of the loop. She had gotten used to seeing small strides and then picking up a new case without ever seeing the ending. A lot of times, the family court held that everything was okay now, no more visits were needed, and that was the end.

But her commitment remained to do as much as she could with the time and tools she had. And she felt she could do so much more out here. See more of the kids, get to know them better, share their successes as well as their problems. Much more personal attention to each child than her job allowed. She needed a more positive environment herself, and she needed to provide a positive environment.

So yes, she was coming back. The question was about right now, and a shaft of anguish that seemed to hold her paralyzed with its force.

Her minefield?

With just those few words, he had skewed her entire self-perception. Her thoughts crawled around, trying to understand what he was talking about and what it meant about her.

God, this was bad. She had to do something. Anything.

Finally she moved, surprised at how much she had stiffened. Hours of sitting caused her body to whimper a minor protest as she stood. Somewhere inside she had been deadened to the passage of time, lost in a maelstrom of emotions and careening thoughts.

She had come out here expecting to say farewell to her aunt and close up the house. She had expected nothing of what had followed, from considering a career change to a major move…and Cliff. She had thought that avenue closed a long time ago. Now it had opened again, just long enough to pierce her.

Downstairs, she made a pot of coffee, certain that she would see the sun rise. Sleep hadn't brushed her with the merest wing in all these hours. Her stomach growled, reminding her that she hadn't eaten, either, but she ignored it.

Martha, never far from her thoughts, returned. Holly could have sworn she felt her aunt sit at the table with her. Could almost smell the lavender sachets she kept in her drawers, a custom Holly had always found quaint and pleasant, but something she had never done herself. A child of the modern age, she used dryer sheets and went around the world with her clothes smelling like nearly everyone else's. But Martha had always smelled of lavender.

God, she wished her aunt were there. That they could have just one more conversation. Their last phone call had been just four days before Martha's stroke. They had laughed. They had talked about Holly's job. Martha had expressed her concern that Holly was sounding awfully tired and needed a break. Holly had promised a visit that summer.

Instead she had come early, to bury Martha. And what had she done with this time, time when she surely should have been grieving and recalling every memory she could about her aunt? Oh, she'd spent some time going through things, but mostly she had hidden from her grief, instead allowing herself to be distracted by planning for a future…and by Cliff.

Had she been hiding in his company to avoid the grief? Maybe. But if so, she'd gotten herself into a fine kettle of fresh pain.

God, she felt filthier than she had after that manhandling by those three guys in Chicago. Never, ever, would she have believed Cliff capable of such cruelty, to make love to her while resuming his relationship with his ex. She might have deserved it, but she had believed it was out of character for him.

She looked at the phone, thinking about calling one of her friends. It might help to talk, but God, it was a conversation she didn't want to have with any one of them. They'd get righteously indignant for her, and that wouldn't help. Or worse, they'd try to make kind excuses, whether for him or her. None of it would mend this pain.

But once she had looked at the phone, she couldn't

stop remembering what Cliff had said about leaving messages. She wasn't sure she wanted to hear them. Her mind was capable of writing the kiss-off. *Thanks for a great lay, but...* Or, *now that Lisa's back....*

Bitterness filled her mouth. But the phone wouldn't leave her alone. The more she tried not to look at it, the more it seemed to pull her gaze. She could almost hear Martha saying one of her favorite phrases, always funny coming out of Martha's mouth: *Man up.*

Boy, how she used to laugh at that, and Martha's brown eyes would sparkle with humor. She could almost see them sparkling at her right now, even though there wasn't one bit of humor in this situation.

So man up, she thought. She probably wouldn't be able to get the messages anyway. That beeping wouldn't tell her how to dial.

But Martha had been meticulous in a lot of ways, and when Holly leaned toward the phone, she saw a list of names, neatly printed, and down near the bottom, next to a button, was *voice mail.*

It couldn't be that easy. Clenching her teeth but deciding to face the music and put an end to at least some of the questions that gnawed at her mind and heart like starving mice, she picked up the receiver and punched the button.

Immediately, she heard a voice say, "Please enter your pass code."

She didn't know the pass code. How would she? Useless. She started to pull the receiver from her ear when she heard a series of five tones. Was it automatically dialing the code?

Apparently so. After another second, the recorded woman's voice spoke again. "Please press one to hear your messages…"

She pressed one and listened. They came to her in reverse order, newest first.

"Holly?" Cliff's voice said. "I'm beginning to worry. Are you okay? You haven't called me back. Did I do something? I hope I can get over there soon. Call me, please."

The second: "I'm sorry I haven't been over. Maybe you can run over here if you want to see the downside of ranching. The lambs are still sick and we're running a twenty-four-hour hospital. Miss you."

And the earliest: "I'm glad you liked the roses. I wish I could get over there, but something's wrong with some of my lambs. It's pretty bad, and we're nursing them. Waiting for the vet. I hope like hell he can figure it out before we start losing them. Call or come over when you can. I miss you."

When she hung up the phone, she felt about two inches tall.

But Lisa said she'd been over there. What the hell had Lisa been doing over there? Not even in her worst imaginings could she believe Cliff would have called her three times, talking about sick lambs, if he was getting back into a relationship with his ex.

Now she had some idea what he had meant by a minefield. Her insides wrenched, nerves made her jump up and she wondered how in the hell she could fix this mess.

Cliff stood by the fold as the sun came up, watching the lambs. They were on their feet again, if a little unsteady, and nursing again. Whatever had hit so many of his lambs hadn't spread any farther. Mike Windwalker, the vet, wasn't sure what had happened, and had sent blood and tissue samples off to a lab somewhere, along with vaccine and wormer samples. Cliff didn't care if the cause had a name, although he supposed it would be good to know whether they'd had a bad reaction to the worming or vaccinations or if they'd had a bug of some kind.

Right now he was just glad they were recovering. Whether that recovery was due to time or the broad-spectrum antibiotics the vet had given them, he hadn't a clue.

He was just glad that nightmare was over. Everyone on the ranch, including Jean, had taken a turn at milking the ewes and trying to bottle-feed the lambs. For a while they'd been too weak to suckle, but when he and his helpers had squeezed the milk into their mouths, at least they had swallowed whatever didn't just run right out.

He should have been shouting hallelujahs. Hell, he'd wanted to share his joy when he'd gone over to see Holly last night. Instead, he'd been treated like a cow patty she wanted to scrape from her boot. Nice.

She'd done that to him once before, but at least he'd understood her reasons last time. This time he didn't care what her reasons might be. He had had enough.

Satisfied that the lambs were continuing to mend, he couldn't squash his anger anymore. Damn woman was a walking honey trap. He'd been the one who had warned her they shouldn't play with fire, then he'd gone right ahead and played with it. Idiot!

Maybe he'd let all that talk about a youth ranch go to his head, thinking she'd actually stay around. Or maybe she'd gotten to his little head. Again. Either way, he was a double-damned idiot.

It was possible that she hadn't recognized that beep on the phone as meaning she had voice mail. He could believe that. Cell phones were different. But not to have called him in all this time, except the once to thank him for the roses? Not to have wondered why he'd just disappeared?

Then to accuse him of getting back together with Lisa? He wasn't capable of two-timing like that, and it infuriated him to know that she thought he could do such a thing.

Damn! He turned from the fold, kicked at a clod of dirt and stomped toward the house. He should have just stuck with his initial impulse to stay away from her, to get the executor stuff done and then drop out of sight. He shouldn't have felt concern for her, shouldn't have worried about how thin and exhausted she looked. None of his business. Her problem, not his. But oh, no, he had to try to help. He had to walk right back into the trap, knowing damn well his attraction to her hadn't faded one teeny little bit. He needed a shrink. Even a native instinct for self-preservation had failed him.

Holly, Holly, Holly. She'd filled his thoughts and made his blood pound when she wasn't even around. Some invisible elastic had kept snapping him back to her side.

He'd thought she had changed. Ha! People didn't change—their faults just became amplified by time, evidently. She couldn't be trusted. And clearly she didn't trust him.

The last thing he needed or wanted to see was Holly coming toward him. She rounded the front of the house and walked toward the fold, catching him between her and the lambs. He almost deviated to the corral to grab a horse and get the hell out of here. He didn't need this. He'd been up all night for too many nights now, and his eyes felt gritty from lack of sleep. Now this?

He passed one of his hired hands. "Keep an eye on

the lambs, will you? And if Lisa shows up looking for a horse, tell her to saddle her own."

The guy's eyes widened. He wasn't used to seeing Cliff angry. "Sure, Boss."

Every damn day he'd had a man pulled away from something more important, namely the sick lambs and herding, to saddle a horse for Lisa. That hadn't changed, either.

Damn all women to hell.

Well, at least Holly didn't look as if she were loaded for bear. Instead what he saw was a tired woman approaching him tentatively. Great, now he was an ogre. He stopped, making her come to him. *Deal with it,* he thought. Just deal with whatever hell she wanted to rain on him and then hit the sack. He could probably sleep for a week.

She halted six feet from him. Much as he wanted to ignore it, he noticed that her eyes looked sunken, her face pale and her mouth unsteady. What now?

"Cliff?"

"My name hasn't changed," he said shortly.

She closed her eyes briefly. "Can we talk?"

"About what? There's nothing left to discuss. You pretty much took care of that last night."

Her mouth quivered. God, not tears. "I got your messages this morning. I'm sorry."

"It's a little late for that."

"Probably. But I owe you an apology. If I had known the lambs were sick I'd have come over to help somehow. I didn't know."

That much he believed. "Okay. Apology accepted." He took a step to walk around her, but she stopped him.

"Cliff, please. We have to talk."

About what? He was tired, he was frustrated, he was

still angry and when he should have been celebrating the recovery of his lambs, all he wanted to do was kill something. "You really don't want to talk to me now."

Her shoulders sagged. Seeing that, something else tried to poke its way through his anger. Concern? No, he wasn't going to step into that mess again.

"Okay," she said quietly. Her head dropped and she started to turn away. He should have let her go. Really he should have. His bed had been calling to him for days now, he was in an awful mood and what good was some talk going to do?

But as always happened with her, he couldn't do it. He couldn't be needlessly cruel, and she had curled in on herself as if he'd just struck her.

"Look," he said, causing her to still, "I'm exhausted, I'm in a hellacious mood and I can't guarantee I can follow a conversation. But okay."

She faced him again, squaring her shoulders as if drawing on every bit of her inner strength. "I messed up. Until last night I hadn't heard from you since the roses. I couldn't imagine why. I must have been out when the phone rang, because I never heard it, and I didn't know about the voice mail. Then when Lisa came back yesterday—she's hardly been there—I asked if she'd found a job. She told me she'd been spending her time with you."

Understanding began to dawn through his anger. "She was spending her time riding my horses." He wouldn't have believed he still had the energy to sound that sarcastic, but sarcasm dripped like hot tar from every word.

"She omitted that part."

"Why am I not surprised." He pulled off his hat, scratched at his head, then clapped it back on. "You believed I would treat you that way?"

She lowered her head, then gave a little nod. "I hadn't heard from you." As if that explained everything.

Not quite, but he guessed if she felt insecure... "Ah, hell," he said finally.

She peeked up at him.

"Quit looking like a whipped dog," he said. "Damn, I've never given you cause to look like this."

"I gave myself cause. I'm embarrassed. Kinda sick, too."

He cussed again, quietly this time, letting go of most of his anger. Okay, they needed to talk. "Remember that old oak by the river?"

She flushed as she nodded, telling him she did indeed remember.

"Let's drive out there."

"Will the lambs be okay?"

"They seem to be getting better faster. I've got enough people to look after them for a few hours. Let's just go where nobody can find us, because I'm getting damn sick of Lisa turning up any time she feels like it. Although I warn you, once we get there I'll probably fall asleep."

There was a wagon track part of the way. Usually they had ridden here, but he didn't have the energy to spare. Driving was his max, and he was grateful the only obstacles were the bumpy ground. At last he pulled up beside the tree.

It was a restful place, although they had seldom been restful for long here that summer. How many times had he tried to tell himself that whole summer had been some kind of aberration? Well, it hadn't been, to judge by the way he'd been reacting to her since she came back.

He grabbed the blanket out of the back and spread it

in the shade. Then he sat, leaning against the trunk and waited for whatever was next, whether it was sleep, a discussion or an argument.

She didn't sit immediately, but stood looking up at the tree with her mouth open. "What happened to the tree?"

He twisted and look up at it. The trunk was split now, but amazingly enough both remaining sides still grew. "Lightning. A week or so after you left last time."

"But it's still alive."

"Incredible, isn't it." Some things never died, he guessed. Maybe they were too strong. Or too stubborn. His head was swimming with fatigue and he didn't even attempt to sort through that thought.

At last she sat on the blanket at the far edge from him. "Sleep if you need to," she said quietly. "I've never seen you so tired."

"Hang around," he tried to joke. "Ranching has this effect sometimes." He wasn't sure all the words emerged, because the tree seemed as comfortable as a pillow and sleep snatched him between one breath and the next.

When he awoke, the shadows had grown shorter and Holly had moved closer to stay in the shade. She was braiding some tall grasses into a long rope, and the sight carried him back a decade in time. She had often liked to do that when they lazed around talking.

But it wasn't ten years ago. It was around noon today, and he still didn't know what he was doing out here with her except that she had wanted to talk. About what, he had no idea. He thought she'd pretty well covered it all already.

He lay still, watching her, thinking about that long-ago summer, thinking about right now. He still felt her pull. In his groin, yes, but other parts of him still wanted her. He might have been the only one of them in love so long ago, but youth notwithstanding, he had loved her.

Some part of his heart and soul wanted to pick up as if a decade had never passed. Well, that wasn't going to happen. They'd been little more than kids then, but they were adults now, and evidently they still had a lot of detritus floating around.

"Thanks for letting me sleep," he said.

She started and twisted toward him. "I'm glad you did. You look better. I needed the time to think, anyway."

He had slipped down while he slept. Now he pushed himself up until he leaned against the tree once more. "There's water in the cooler in the back of my truck. It's probably warm, but you must be thirsty by now."

She dropped her braiding and jumped up, returning quickly with a bottle of water for each of them. Then she sat cross-legged, facing him. Leaves tossed in a gentle breeze, causing sun and shadow to dance across her face.

"I hope you got some sleep," he said. Because she still looked hollow.

"A little. Thanks. What was wrong with the lambs?"

"We're still not sure. Waiting for test results."

"But they're okay now?"

"A whole lot better. For a couple of days, I thought I was going to lose a whole bunch of them."

"That must have been scary."

"It was," he admitted. "For a while they were even too weak to suckle, so we milked the ewes and used bottles to squeeze some nourishment into them. But it's better. They started standing again yesterday, and by late afternoon they were suckling again. So they made it."

"I'm so glad." She picked up the braid and fiddled with the end of it. "I would have helped if I had known. Really."

"I admit I was kind of surprised you never popped over."

She bit her lip. "I hate to imagine what you were thinking of me."

"Nothing near as bad as what you evidently thought of me."

Her cheeks reddened and her head dipped. "When you didn't call...well, when I didn't know you'd been calling, I kind of thought the roses were a kiss-off. A way of getting even for how I hurt you that summer."

"God!" He sat up a little straighter. "And then Lisa."

"Yeah. And then Lisa."

He mulled that around. "Have people been treating you that badly?"

"As a rule, no." She raised her head, met his gaze, then looked away again. "You have no idea what I see on a regular basis. I know what people are capable of, Cliff. A lot of it isn't pretty."

"So it's affected your expectations?"

"I think it's made me more defensive, yes. And apparently more suspicious."

"Damn, woman, you need a new job."

"Yes, I think I do."

Fully awake now, he leaned forward until his elbows rested on his folded knees. "You've made up your mind?"

"Well, when I wasn't busy imagining the worst, I started making some phone calls. A friend from Chicago wants to help me. She's a family psychologist and says she'll work for room and board. And I talked to the lawyer, Mr. Carstairs. He's looking into all the legal aspects, but he seems to think that I should start as a guest ranch. I can invite families out here. It'll get me up and running while we deal with all the stuff having just the kids here would require. So I think I'll do that. I can afford to bring some families out here, thanks to Aunt Martha."

"That sounds like a good plan."

She nodded. "I need to go back for maybe a month to close up everything. My cases, my apartment, giving notice, all that. But then I'm coming back here for good."

"In spite of me."

"In spite of you," she agreed. "My mind is made up."

"Good." He honestly meant it. The last thing he wanted was for her to move here because of him. He couldn't think of a worse reason.

He could see that wasn't the answer she had hoped for, but it was the only honest one he could give her. She had to decide to live here for her own reasons. Anything else could be poisonous, and she had herself to thank for teaching him that lesson. It had taken awhile after she left, but he'd finally gotten it.

She picked at the braided grass she held, then slowly started weaving again. "I bet this stuff with the lambs put a hole in your budget."

The change of direction surprised him. "Temporarily. We'll catch up soon. We'll be selling wool and lambs before long."

"Good."

Man, this was getting awkward. She clearly needed to say something more and couldn't find her way to it. Or couldn't find the words. But he couldn't stay out here all day waiting. He needed to get back, spell his guys so they could catch some sleep and check on those lambs again. Ten years ago, his parents had pretty much let him have huge chunks of time over the summer to go running around with Holly, but he was the one in charge now. He couldn't afford to be so careless.

At last Holly broke the silence. "I'm leaving tomorrow."

His stomach took a plunge. He swilled some water before trying to reply. "I thought you had a few more days."

"I do. But I'm trying to change my flight. If I can't, well, a few days in Denver won't hurt. There's a lot I need to think about."

"I thought you'd made up your mind?"

Her brows lifted. "I have. I'm coming back. But for some reason being in Martha's house isn't helping, being around you isn't helping and I need to clear out some cobwebs. This is a huge leap I'm about to make, and I need some space to be perfectly clear in my own head." Then she smiled. "I also need to talk to some people. I'm getting impatient to get rolling."

That smile was heartbreakingly beautiful, he thought. Then she jumped up, wiped her hands on her jeans and said, "I imagine you need to get back. I'll leave Lisa the house keys, and tell her to give them back to you when she's ready to move on."

Just like that. He drove her back to her car, she paused just long enough to squeeze his hand, then she drove away.

He felt as if he'd just been hit by a truck, though he

wasn't sure why. She'd said she was coming back. But why the hell was she leaving so early?

To get away from him?

Damn, he was feeling angry all over again.

Chapter Eleven

A month later when Holly walked up the Jetway in Denver, she could feel a spring in her step. A month had done wonders. She'd handed off her cases, easing the transition for her families. She'd found lots of interest and support inside the department and outside among charities in her idea for the ranch and she even had some commitments for donations once the place opened.

She'd put on five pounds while she was at it. And this time she wasn't coming to bury her aunt. No, she'd spent plenty of time in the past month saying farewell in a way she hadn't seemed able to do while staying at Martha's house: she had remembered. Somehow the indulgence of endless hours of remembering her aunt had brought her to a sense of peace. She still missed Martha, missed her deeply, but now it was a quieter, more comfortable grief, one she didn't keep trying to hide from by distracting herself the way she had during the time she had spent in Wyoming. She had faced it, and accepted it.

Maybe most importantly, she had felt an opening inside herself, a welcoming for whatever the future might hold. Yes, she'd been excited by the idea of all this before, but there'd been plenty of trepidation and uncertainty, even once she made up her mind. There would always be uncertainty of some kind, but she had emerged from her internal mental crouch and felt ready to open her arms to all the experiences life might bring.

So she was already smiling when she saw Cliff waiting for her once she left the security area behind. The cobwebs of the past no longer seemed to cloud her vision.

He returned her smile and held up a single long-stemmed rose.

For another year, she thought, and her throat tightened even as happiness bubbled up in her. She didn't know what was going to happen between them. The years had changed them, and the little time they'd had together had probably only shown her part of the man he'd become. One thing for certain, she knew she was a different person from just one month ago.

When she reached him, he caught her in a bear hug and kissed her soundly. "Welcome home," he said as he released her. Then he handed her the rose. "You look wonderful."

"So do you," she said frankly. "Thank you for the rose. It's beautiful. Now let's blow this joint. I hate airports."

He laughed and grabbed her carry-on. "You must have checked bags."

"I shipped some boxes yesterday. I decided Martha had the right idea—go minimalist."

"So what's all the news?" he asked as they worked their way through passengers and courtesy carts. Even though they had talked weekly on the phone during the past month, they'd avoided heavy emotional ground. She had talked about her job and her plans, he had talked about ranching. The only thing he had left her really sure about was that he wasn't angry anymore. They had become friends at last.

"Well, I got myself squared away, I think."

"Meaning?"

She glanced at him from the corner of her eye, wishing it was possible to just stare at him. He was certainly stareworthy. "I cleaned the cobwebs out of the attic. Let's just get out of here. There must be some place less hectic to have coffee and talk."

"I had bigger plans," he admitted. "How do you feel about staying in town overnight before we head back?"

How did she feel? Like a rocket being launched. Capable of dancing on air. *My God,* she thought, it had been a long time since she had felt this happy just to be alive. And to be with Cliff?

She cautioned herself to hold her horses. She had no idea whether he wanted anything from her beyond neighborly friendship. "I'd love it," she responded, hoping she sounded like it without letting her elation seep out with every word.

He took them into town, locating a coffee shop that didn't seem too busy. He ordered espresso, and she ordered a gloriously sinful mocha frappé. They sat outside, enjoying the early-summer warmth and a pleasant breeze.

"First you," she said. "How are the lambs and how is business?"

"Everything's doing great. Thank God the vet is attentive to detail. He marked down the vaccine lots he gave the sheep, and the fifteen who got sick all got the same lot, a different one from the other lambs. Apparently the bacteria in the vaccine was live and kicking, instead of being properly weakened. It's probably going to cause a major recall."

"So you made your lambs sick by trying to help them? That must burn."

"I'm just glad it didn't spread past them. It could have, and I wouldn't have been able to nurse hundreds of lambs. Anyway, we're doing great, we got some pretty decent prices on the wool and on the lambs we sold. We're set for another year, and we should have some more angora wool to sell this fall. You could say things are looking up."

"I'm glad." She meant it from the bottom of her heart, and found herself wishing they weren't in such a public place. She might have cleared out the cobwebs in her brain, but not her attraction to Cliff. Just sitting across from him like this made her insides clench with need.

"Now you," he said.

"Well, I got a lot of positive feedback on my ranch idea, and some charities have promised to donate once I get it started."

"Super." He smiled. "That must make you feel good."

"It does. Things are looking up." She hesitated, aware that her heart was beating nervously. The other things were harder to discuss. A lot harder. "I took time to grieve for Martha. I wasn't doing that when I was here. I was finding every excuse to avoid it. Somehow it was easier to do back in Chicago. I don't know why."

"Maybe because you weren't surrounded by constant

reminders. I don't know, but it seems to me being in her house was like being caught between two realities."

"That's a good way to describe it, I think. Some part of me just didn't seem capable of accepting that she was gone." Sighing, she looked down. "It was a helluva month, Cliff. It was a week before I decided to turn in my resignation. It was like giving up a huge chunk of who I was. But once I did it, I felt light enough to float. So I guess I'd reached my limit. Everyone was very understanding, and reminded me that caseworkers have a limited life expectancy. We see too much sadness, pain and ugliness. As one of them said to me, I'd have had to kill my emotions not to care that much, and when you care that much…well, finally things inside you start to shut down because you can't handle any more. That wouldn't have been good, and I was getting there."

He nodded encouragingly.

"Some things you said also helped."

"Me?" He appeared surprised.

"Yeah, just little things, but they made me step back and take a look at myself. I was living in what I think of as a mental crouch. I had gotten to the point of expecting the worst of everyone, Cliff. I don't want to live that way, but that's what I was doing. So I hammered away at that some, and managed to mostly shake it off. There are lots of good people in the world. I need to spend more time with them."

"I'm so glad."

She met his turquoise gaze and saw real pleasure there. And the sparkle of something hotter, something that had never died between them. Her body responded instantly. That, she thought, would probably never change. But where would it take them?

All of a sudden she wanted to blow this joint, too.

* * *

"I only reserved one room," he said as they approached the hotel.

"That's fine," she managed. Her heart had begun to hammer with anticipation and even some anxiety, and it had risen to clog her throat. Her core began to throb as if climax was only moments away. She would never understand this chemistry between them.

"I can get another…"

She interrupted. "Oh, cut it out. No more games."

He laughed, but the sound was husky. "I know. Somehow we need to slow down. Maybe talk, fool around, that thing they call foreplay."

"I always like it better after."

At that a loud crack of laughter escaped him and despite her anticipation and nerves, a grin stretched her own cheeks until they nearly hurt.

She'd expected a relatively cheap motel, but instead he took her to a real hotel, a nice one, the kind where a bellman took their bags. The part of her that had been scraping by for so long made her wonder if he could afford this. On the other hand, he had chosen it, and as she had already learned, he was no spendthrift.

She expressed her amazement and appreciation when they reached their room, which was not only lovely but had a great view of the Denver skyline. "I feel like a princess!" she exclaimed.

"I hope you always do."

Her breath caught and she turned to him. "Cliff?"

"That's still my name." But there was no smile as he closed the space between them and took her into his arms. Feeling him snugly against her reminded her how much she had been missing him. And for how long? Ten years. Ever since she had left him the first time.

She'd had a mission, but in giving him up, she'd given up something very important.

Only now could she truly face that. Maybe she had done the right thing. She had certainly done what she was determined to do. Maybe everything had happened the way it was supposed to, but it remained that she had never stopped missing him.

"I could jump you right now," he said quietly. "But you know what? We both need more than that. We know that part is great. This time, damn it, I want us to share other things."

She remembered those lazy conversations that had always followed their sex. It wasn't as though they hadn't talked. They'd talked volumes during the afterglow. She remembered a summer of laughter, love and talk. Everything had clicked in its own time and way.

But that was ten years ago, so maybe he was right. Maybe they needed a different approach.

She sat at the table near the window while he called room service and ordered some food. "I'm sure the peanuts on the airplane weren't enough," he said as he joined her at the table.

"I've been eating more," she admitted.

"I can tell and it looks great. I was worried about you when you arrived last month."

"I didn't exactly realize it, but I guess I was worried about me, too."

He reached across the table and took both her hands. "I've been thinking."

"Yes?" She wondered if that was a good thing or a bad thing. All of a sudden she didn't feel like jumping for joy.

"I want to help you realize your youth ranch. I may not be able to help much financially, but I'm sure my men and I can help with construction and that kind of thing. Is that okay with you?"

"Of course." But the lump remained in her throat.

He smiled faintly. "Good. But there's more. If there's one thing I figured out when you were here, it's that I'm not over you. I thought I was, but I'm sure as hell not. The thing is, we can't pick up where we left off ten years ago. We're not the same people. So unless you object, I want to pick up here and now. I want to date you, I want to spend time with you. I want us to learn who we are now."

"I'd like that."

"I can learn all about what you do and want to do. You can get an understanding of what I do and why there might be long stretches when you hardly see me. We can find out if we mesh. I think we probably will, though."

"Why?"

"Because we're going to both be ranchers, even if different kinds."

Despite her nervousness, she had to laugh. It was true in its own way.

"The thing is, Holly, I'm pretty sure I'm still in love with you. So I don't want you to go forward on this with me unless you're pretty sure you might fall in love with me. I don't need a rerun of what happened before. So I guess what I'm asking is, blow me off now, because you might not be able to blow me off later. And we're going to be neighbors for a long, long time. There are limits to my masochism."

That was fair, she thought as he went to answer the door for room service, even though her heart wanted to sing at his declaration of love. Soon enough a tray of hors d'oeuvres occupied the table along with tall icy glasses of tea. Cliff rejoined her and encouraged her to eat.

But eating was the last thing she seemed capable of doing just then. "I think," she said slowly, "that I'm still in love with you, too. I didn't want to face it. I never wanted to face it. I was too driven, and then I had to believe I made the right decision."

"I think you did," he said, surprising her. "We were just kids. Honestly, if you hadn't dumped me, but had stayed, you'd probably have resented me. I get it. It was the wrong time, if nothing else. Maybe this won't turn out to be the right time, either."

"I'm not so sure about that." *Screw the food,* she thought. She rose and went around the table. He instinctively pulled back and she perched on his lap.

"You're striking matches again," he warned her.

"We always strike matches. Get used to it. It's who we are, at least together. What else do you want from me?"

"I'd like to have kids eventually."

"I love kids." She smiled. She wasn't sure who was moving, but their mouths were getting closer together, then his hand ran up her back.

"Not yet, though," he said quickly. "We need to date for a while."

"I already agreed to that. A year?"

He blinked. "A year?"

"Sure. I want a June wedding. And neither of us will be able to say we didn't know what we were getting into after a year."

He laughed, then scooped her up and carried her straight to the bed. "You drive me out of my mind."

"I have no mind when it comes to you."

It happened as it always happened, fast and furious. Some people might consider their lovemaking to be backward, but not them. In the afterglow they shared the caresses and gentle explorations, the absolute knowledge of one another's bodies. And the passion built again.

"A year?" he said dubiously.

"A year," she repeated, sounding more certain than she felt.

"Damn," he muttered, just before he buried his head between her thighs and lashed her with his tongue to the highest pinnacle.

A year, she thought before all reason fled. It was going to be a great year.

Epilogue

Holly stood on the porch and looked out over the huge crowd that filled Cliff's ranch. She was happy, truly happy, and hugged herself.

Cliff had joked that they should get married on their flat rock. She had pointed out that it would be impossible to invite guests to attend there, and anyway, she wanted that rock to be their secret. Then he'd suggested their favorite tree. She'd simply looked at him until he laughed.

So here they were, married in his pasture, throwing a barbecue-cum-potluck for everyone who wanted to attend. It seemed most of the county had turned out.

She had also invited the three families who were now staying at her ranch in the three cabins Cliff had helped her build. They'd completed the structures last fall and spent the winter fixing them up inside.

Despite her fears that her families might be ignored,

lots of people had welcomed them warmly, and their kids were enjoying horseback rides under the care of Cliff's hired hands and a few volunteers.

Children ran everywhere, screeching, laughing and having a great time. It was the happiest day ever. Her soul felt good and her heart filled to the brim with joy.

Strong arms closed around her from behind, probably crushing the back of her wedding dress, but she didn't care.

He pushed her short veil aside and nuzzled her neck. "How are you doing, Mrs. Martin?"

"I've never been happier, Mr. Martin."

He chuckled. "You never answered on the name thing."

"Right now I'll enjoy being Mrs."

He gave a pretend sigh. "Then comes Ms. I knew it."

She giggled.

"How's Junior?"

"Cliff! We don't know yet." She had just found out she was pregnant.

"I know, and I'm going to love it, girl or boy. But dang, it's hard to call it *it*."

She laughed again. "*Baby* will do."

He squeezed her gently. "You've made me the happiest man on earth. And look at your families. Folks are being nice."

"I was a little nervous about it."

"I know you were. But we're a hospitable people for the most part. And asking for volunteers instead of wedding gifts was genius on my part."

She turned within the circle of his arms. His eyes were bright and happier than she had ever seen them, except possibly when she had told him they were pregnant. "What?"

He reached in the back pocket of his slacks and pulled out an envelope. "Jean's been collecting them. Take a look."

She opened the envelope eagerly and pulled out a stack of neatly folded typed pages.

Gene Winters—construction
Marybelle Jasper—gardening
Susan Peabody—sewing
Ransom Laird—livestock
Gideon Ironheart—trail rides/horse training

She stopped reading and looked up as tears sparkled in her eyes. "Oh, Cliff…"

"I know. I think you'll find all bases covered. There are some teachers in there, people from the college, promises to provide feed for the animals, free vet care…. You're off and running, Holly. A whole lot of people are behind you on this."

"Wow," she whispered. "Just wow." She lifted her arms and threw them around his neck. "It's a dream come true!"

Applause started somewhere out in the pasture and swiftly swelled.

"I think they want us to kiss," Cliff said, his eyes sparkling.

"I don't think we can light a match right now."

"Obviously not. Can't even escape because we postponed our honeymoon. But dang, we can give them a kiss to remember."

Which is exactly what they did.

* * * * *

COMING NEXT MONTH FROM

H HARLEQUIN

SPECIAL EDITION

Available February 18, 2014

#2317 LASSOED BY FORTUNE
The Fortunes of Texas: Welcome to Horseback Hollow
by Marie Ferrarella
Liam Jones doesn't want any part of newfound Fortune relatives—or the changes they bring to Horseback Hollow. *He's crazy,* thinks Julia Tierney. The ambitious beauty was always the one Liam could never snag in high school. When Julia becomes the chef at a local restaurant, Julia and Liam find that old attractions die hard....

#2318 THE DADDY SECRET
Return to Brighton Valley • by Judy Duarte
When Mallory Dickinson gave up her son, she never thought she'd see Brighton Valley—or her baby's father, Rick Martinez—again. A decade later, she's back in town with her son, whom she adopted—and Rick's become a responsible veterinarian. Can the former bad boy and the social worker let their guards down to allow love in?

#2319 A PROPOSAL AT THE WEDDING
Bride Mountain • by Gina Wilkins
Father-of-the-bride Paul Brennan can't help but find himself tempted by irresistible innkeeper Bonnie Carmichael. Trouble arises, though, since Bonnie hopes to create a life and family at Bride Mountain Inn, and Paul's already done fatherhood. In the shadow of Bride Mountain, love blooms as they find their way to a happily-ever-after.

#2320 FINDING FAMILY...AND FOREVER?
The Bachelors of Blackwater Lake • by Teresa Southwick
Kidnapped as a child, Emma Robbins heads to Blackwater Lake to find her birth family. In the process, she becomes the nanny to Dr. Justin Flint's young son. The handsome widower is unwillingly attracted to the lovely newcomer, who loves the boy as her own, but secrets and lies may undermine the family they begin to build.

#2321 HER ACCIDENTAL ENGAGEMENT • by Michelle Major
Single mom Julia Morgan needs a man—not for love, but to keep custody of her son, Charlie. Local police chief Sam Callahan wants to keep his family out of his love life. The two engage in a romance of convenience, but what begins as a pretense might just evolve into true love.

#2322 THE ONE HE'S BEEN LOOKING FOR • by Joanna Sims
World-renowned photographer Ian Sterling is going blind, and he wants to find the model of his dreams before he loses his sight entirely. He finds his muse in rebellious Jordan Brand, but there's more than a camera between these two. To truly heal, Ian must open his heart to see what's been in front of him all along.

YOU CAN FIND MORE INFORMATION ON UPCOMING HARLEQUIN® TITLES, FREE EXCERPTS AND MORE AT WWW.HARLEQUIN.COM.

HSECNM0214

REQUEST YOUR FREE BOOKS!
2 FREE NOVELS PLUS 2 FREE GIFTS!

⟨H⟩ HARLEQUIN®

SPECIAL EDITION
Life, Love & Family

When Mallory Dickinson is reunited with her first love, she has to decide whether to tell him her deepest secret—that her young son is his biological child!

***

Mallory took a deep breath, probably trying to gather her thoughts—or maybe to lie.

But it didn't take a brain surgeon to see the truth. She'd kept the baby she was supposed to have given up for adoption, and she'd let ten years go by without telling Rick.

Betrayal gnawed at his gut.

"Lucas called you a doctor," she said, arching a delicate brow.

"I'm a veterinarian. My clinic is just down the street."

As she mulled that over, Lucas sidled up to Rick wearing a bright-eyed grin. "Did you come to ask my mom about Buddy?"

No, the dog was the last thing he'd come to talk to Mallory about. And while he hadn't been sure just how the conversation was going to unfold when he arrived, it had just taken a sudden and unexpected turn.

"Why would he come to talk to me about his dog?" Mallory asked her son.

Or rather *their* son. Who else could the boy be?

Lucas, who wore a smile that indicated he was completely oblivious to the tension building between the adults, approached Mallory. "Because Buddy needs a home. Since we have a yard now, can I have him? *Please?* I promise to take care of him and walk him and everything."

She said, "We'll talk about it later."

"Okay. Thanks." He flashed Rick a smile, then turned and headed toward the stairs.

As Lucas was leaving, Rick's gaze traveled from the boy to Mallory and back again. Finally, when they were alone, Rick folded his arms across his chest, shifted his weight to one hip and smirked.

"Cute kid," he said.

Mallory flushed brighter still, and she wiped her palms along her hips.

Nervous, huh? Rick's internal B.S. detector slipped into overdrive.

Well, she ought to be.

When Rick had found out about her pregnancy, he'd been only seventeen, but he'd offered to quit school, get a job and marry her. However, her grandparents had decided that she was too young and convinced her that adoption was the only way to go. So they'd sent her to Boston to live with her aunt Carrie until the birth.

Yet in spite of what she'd promised him when she left, she hadn't come back to Brighton Valley. And within six months' time, he'd lost all contact with her—through no fault of his own.

Apparently, she'd had a change of heart about the adoption. And about the feelings she'd claimed she'd had for him, too.

***

Enjoy this sneak peek from USA TODAY *bestselling author Judy Duarte's* THE DADDY SECRET, *the first book in* RETURN TO BRIGHTON VALLEY, *a brand-new miniseries coming in March 2014!*